SHEER TERROR.

The trail was impossible and even the thought of a leap off the sheer drop made Poco almost sick. The wind was swooping down from the peaks, pressing him against the wall. Poco rose, Cardowan a second behind him.

"Let's go," Poco said.

Cardowan said nothing, watching him. Poco reached under his sorrel's neck to sweep in the reins. . . . And in that moment, Cardowan struck the three matches he had in his hand on the rock and when they were mounting into full flare, he jabbed them into the sorrel's rump, at the same time hugging the wall.

The sorrel yanked his head up, exploded ahead, smashing into Poco, a squeal welling in its throat. Poco made one frantic grab as he felt himself off balance, and then the sorrel rocketed by him, butting him with a terrific impact. And in that one brief half-second of cold horror in which he clawed at the air, he heard Cardowan's laugh rise on the wind.

Luke Short Novels:

Bought with a Gun
Bounty Guns
Brand of Empire
The Branded Man
King Colt
The Man on the Blue
Marauders' Moon
Raw Land
Savage Range

BOLD
RIDER

Luke Short

A DELL BOOK

Published by
Dell Publishing
a division of
Bantam Doubleday Dell Publishing Group, Inc.
666 Fifth Avenue
New York, New York 10103

ISBN: 0-440-10683-4

Reprinted by arrangement with The Estate of
Frederick D. Glidden

Printed in the United States of America

Published simultaneously in Canada

New Dell Edition

April 1989

10 9 8 7 6 5 4 3 2 1

KRI

CHAPTER ONE

Back and forth in the rocky valley of Polvosa a lazy dry wind shuttled. Starting from the south slope in a tall and invisible funnel, it idled down to the valley floor, rolled across the railroad spur that led into Christian City, flattened out into a ground sweep, and rode a curling plume of dirt and tumble weeds into the town.

Getting a grip on the powdered dust of the wide main street, it raised a tall dust devil which it dragged the length of the town. Skittering down the shallow canyon between the weathered falsefront buildings, it forced the hipshot saddled horses at the tie rails to saw over on the other hip and close their eyes. It stirred the batwing door of the Sunflower Saloon, caromed off the next buildings and swept out of town and over the bridge.

The stream beneath the plank bridge it ignored and raced up the north slope of the valley in a whistling gust. Almost to the summit it was nearing the road when a horseman at a hard gallop topped the ridge, and in another moment slanted down into its blinding maelstrom of driven sand.

He was through it in two seconds, but when he emerged he was hatless. He did not even look back. The leggy sorrel under him was patched with sweat and dust, and worked with a kind of coasting weariness as he took the downgrade to the bridge. Approaching the thick timber of the bridge, the rider pulled the sorrel into a trot and reined off the road to the river bank.

It was a steep slope down, perhaps twelve feet.

The rider said, "Take it."

The sorrel yawed a couple of times, then squatted on his haunches, spread his forelegs and went over in a rush of

small rock and dirt that slopped into the shallow creek on
the heel of the rocketing splash. The weight of a bigger
man would have foundered the sorrel, but it pulled out
of the slide shaking its head and answered to the rein that
guided it into the black block of shadow under the bridge.

Stopped, the sorrel shook its head and lowered it to
drink, and it got two mouthfuls before it was pulled up.

"Easy," the rider said gently.

Observed now, there was a curious contradiction in
this man. He could hear the thundering racket of many
horses coming down the hardpacked hill road he had
just left and he looked at his small browned hand holding
the reins where a dribble of dust was already sifting down
from the vibrating bridge planks above him. Yet there
was no excitement, no relief in his eyes, in his face. He
was young, under middle height, and now he stretched
and yawned with an indolent economy of movement that
was as clean and alert and contained as a cat's. Finished,
he began unbuttoning the gaudy red shirt he wore. He
pulled the tails out of his trousers just as the thunder hit
the bridge above, and even then he did not pause, only
said, "Steady," to his sorrel while he took off his shirt.

When he twisted around in the saddle to untie his lean
duffle bag, the pennants of dust had powdered his thick
chestnut hair and shoulders. He yawned again. Naked
from the waist up now, he was again a contradiction, for
he looked larger, far solider. His bones were small, his
shoulders capped with a deep roll of muscle that coiled
and sawed with every finger movement. The chest was
deep, high, a dead white against the tanned V of his neck
which itself was scarcely darker than his still, lean, smooth
face. There was a kind of brooding and somnolent arrogance in his face, too, as if all this he was doing and was
about to do was a faintly unpleasant task. His eyes, dark
to blackness and set deep and wide in his skull, were pleasantly mocking, amused.

From his bag he drew out a clean blue shirt and put it
on. As soon as it was buttoned, he stuffed the red shirt in
the bag and tied the bag behind the cantle.

Now he said again to the sorrel, "Steady," and drew his feet from the stirrups. Gingerly he stood up on the saddle and reached for a bridge beam overhead. Once he had steadied himself, he used his free hand to tuck in his shirt-tail, to ram it down past the shell belt and sagging holster from which a worn cedar-handled Colt jutted.

Satisfied, he put his other hand on the bridge beam and swung clear of the saddle. He spoke to the horse which turned upstream and began walking the creek. Soon it was lost from sight around the bend.

Left hanging, the man did a handover to the edge of the bridge where this beam jutted out to form a support for the railing.

Then he swung himself up and looked down the road. In the street of the town a hundred yards down the road, he could see the blue uniforms of the cavalry troop still mounted. He smiled fleetingly and sat down on the beam jut again and built a cigarette with deft, absent fingers. He had smoked it down when he heard again the thunder of the horses approaching.

Smashing out the cigarette, he put the butt in his shirt pocket, then swung down again under the bridge, travelled the beam a yard, then swung up again in the space between the joist and planks.

This time the horses pulled up on the bridge.

A man's voice said suddenly, "Look at that bank, Lieutenant!"

"Took to the water, huh?" another man said gruffly. "All right, we'll do the same."

"That's a hell of a drop," the first man said.

There was a pause in the conversation, then the lieutenant said, "Take the other bank. It flattens out down there forty yards or so each way."

"Up or down?"

"We'll split. Take half the men, Sergeant. Put at least two in the creek and the rest of you ride the bank. I'll do the same."

"Yes, sir. How far?"

"Till you get him," the lieutenant said curtly.

There was more thunder of horses turning around on the planks. The ten troopers split and half went east, the other half west, some in the creek, the others riding the bank.

As soon as they were out of sight, the slight figure swung up onto the bridge and headed for town, brushing his clothes off with quick, flicking, absent movements.

There was no haste in his walk; neither was there any halting stiffness likely to be bred by the high heels of his neat halfboots and by hours in the saddle.

Looking up he saw there was no unusual movement of people on the main street, which indicated the townsfolk did not share the army's joy of pursuit. He built another cigarette and lighted it just as he hit the boardwalk of town.

Shouldering through the doors of the Sunflower Saloon, he walked straight to the bar. The room was not crowded, a dozen men at the gambling tables, four or five at the bar. All talk, even the click of poker chips, ceased at his entrance. The fat and placid-looking bartender saw him, smiled uneasily, and said, "Just a moment, Poco."

He climbed up on the back bar, reached up above the mirror and took down a large picture of a nude woman stretched languorously and astonishingly on a vista of green lawn. He put the picture under the bar and said diffidently in the continuing silence, "I've kep' it from bein' shot up so far. What'll it be?"

"Beer," the slight man said, and added, "Did the army leave a hat here?"

The bartender nodded quickly and looked up at him. "Oh, so you're the—"

"Yes," the man cut in in a soft voice. "The hat."

The barkeep went up front and came back with a worn, dust-colored Stetson which he tendered the small man. About to speak, the bartender glanced over the man's shoulder and saw a puncher heading stealthily for the door.

"You," the barkeep called.

The puncher stopped dead in his tracks and looked

guiltily at the barkeep.

"If you tell the marshal he's here," the bartender said slowly, "you'll pay for every smashed mirror and window and chair in the bar. And if *I* got anything to say about it, you'll pay for the marshal's buryin' too."

"Not me," the puncher said quickly, earnestly. "Hell, all I want to do is get out of town."

The slight man's gaze sought the puncher's in the mirror. "Sit down," he drawled quietly. "Nothing's going to happen."

"Yes, *sir*," the puncher said and tiptoed back to his seat.

The slight man sipped his beer when it came, his eyes dreamy, indifferent. The sodden silence he ignored, as if used to it. But he was not so unobserving that he missed the movement behind him when a man got up from a poker table and crossed to the bar beside him.

This man was tall, made taller by the gambler's black frockcoat which he wore. He ordered a bourbon and looked at the slight man, and over his thin, handsome and amiable face came an amused look. Under the wide black mustache, he smiled a little. "Hello, Poco. Trouble?"

"No," the slight man said.

"You took long enough," the gambler growled.

Poco said nothing, only studied the man in the mirror. Two-Way Hornbeck, at present dressed in the tradition of only one of his dozen callings, was probably the royalty of riff-raff. Most towns in the southwest knew him, usually to their sorrow and his advantage. Suave, dark of face, hard of eye, ready of smile, he had the agreeable and expansive presence of the generous rich. Years sat on him with such grace that Poco had never tried to guess his age, but had merely accepted him as permanent.

Two-Way accepted Poco's scrutiny with a smile. "I've got a room upstairs. Ten's the number. Go on up."

"Go 'way," Poco said gently.

Two-Way scowled. "Go on up. I've been waiting for—"

"Go 'way," Poco said, without even looking at him.

Two-Way backed off and returned to his table. Poco saw him writing something on a slip of paper, then he called the bartender for drinks. In another moment the bartender laid a note on the bar in front of Poco. Poco drew a match out of his pocket, struck it, touched it to the unread note and dropped it burning into a spittoon. He finished his beer and went out.

Stopping in front of the batwing doors, he looked up and down the street, surveying the town. There was no interest in his still face, nothing except a mild and patient curiosity. He was wondering if his sorrel had had time enough to circle back to the feed stable.

A voice from behind him said, "A quarter of a million dollars. How does it sound?"

Poco St. Vrain turned slowly. Two-Way Hornbeck was standing beside him, smiling.

Poco said gently, flatly, "Have I got to cuff you?"

Under his gaze, Two-Way's smile faded. He took a step to the rear until his back was against one of the batwing doors. "Now listen, Poco. Hear it out, anyway," he pleaded softly. "Two hundred and fifty thousand dollars."

Poco uncrossed his arms and rubbed his side with one hand. When his fingers crossed the shellbelt above the holster, Two-Way dived inside the saloon.

Poco turned and walked toward the livery stable, proclaimed so by a huge sign. He was about to swing under the tie-rail and cross to it when he saw three men come down off the hotel porch and turn his way. He paused, hands on hips, watching them.

They were engaged in conversation, two of the men listening to the rumbling, perorated speech of the man in the middle. He was a vast man, a head taller than the two tall punchers at his side, clothed in a baggy and shapeless black suit that fitted him like the skin of a bear. Under his black Stetson his white hair tufted out. Everything about him bespoke dominance, power, even to the polite attentiveness of the men listening to him.

Poco watched their approach, standing motionless himself, a faint unpleasant smile on his face.

In the midst of his speech, the big man looked up, and when he saw Poco he stopped, and his talk trailed off. The two punchers looked up. When they saw Poco their faces were utterly readable. They stepped away from their companion and waited. One of them licked his lips.

The big man's face lost its look of assurance.

"Get off the walk, McCandless," Poco drawled gently. "Can't you see I'm on it?"

Under McCandless's coat twin shellbelts were crossed, dragged slanting by his guns. But it was as if he were unaware he had them.

He said, "Is this it, St. Vrain?" and he could not fight out the torment in his voice.

"Not yet, Abe. Get off the walk."

McCandless stopped. Poco swung under the hitchrack and headed down and across the street for the livery stable. McCandless, his two men trailing him, came out into the road. Poco glanced at them briefly, unsmiling, and went his way. McCandless and his two companions stepped up on the walk where Poco had been standing. The big man paused, looked back at Poco's vanishing figure and drew a handkerchief from his hip pocket, with which he wiped his face thoroughly, his hands a little unsteady.

An old man sat in a backtilted chair just inside the arch of the feed stable.

Poco asked him, "Did a saddled sorrel drift in here?"

The man nodded. "He yours?"

Poco nodded too.

"Prove it."

"He's branded Bullseye on the left hip."

"So's a lot of horses."

Poco shifted to the other foot. "He tied?"

"No. I unsaddled him and rubbed him down and watered and fed him. He's a good horse. Prove he's yours."

Poco whistled a low note twice. In a moment the sorrel walked out of the gloom of the stall toward him.

"Go back," Poco said.

The sorrel turned and went back.

"What do I owe you?" Poco said.

The old man told him, chuckling over his own contrariness. Poco gave him a coin and he went in to change it. Poco stepped out into the sun, letting it warm his back.

Then he heard someone say, "Just listen to me, Poco. Just listen. A quarter million dollars. Think of it!"

Poco started to turn when the voice, Two-Way's voice, said, "Stand still, you damn fool! I've got a gun on you. You've *got* to listen."

Still Poco turned. Two-Way was just inside the door, his back to a stall partition, a gun in his unsteady hand.

Poco walked slowly over to him and reached out and took the gun and dropped it on the floor, and there was no surprise or anger in his face, only impatience.

"When you do that to me, Two-Way, it's time to ride."

"I know it," Two-way said huskily. "But can't you see I'm desperate? Do you think I'd of done that if I wasn't?"

Poco said nothing for a minute, and then he said, "No."

"Will you come up to my room, then?"

"Lead off," Poco said.

"No. Not together," Two-Way said hurriedly. "I'll go up. You follow in a minute. Ten's the number. Up those back stairs in the Sunflower." Then he changed his mind. "No. You go in the hotel next door and get a room. Jacob Finger is your name. I'll be up soon."

"No."

"Why not?"

"Say it here."

"I can't! You know that. I can't, I tell you! I'll go get a room. It'll be on the second floor. I'll be there."

Before Poco could say anything, Two-Way had gone. The stableman came out with Poco's change and Poco told him he'd be after his horse in a little while. He gave Two-Way a couple of minutes, then walked down the street and entered the hotel.

CHAPTER TWO

Two-Way was waiting at the head of the stairwell and he led the way down the corridor to a room. In spite of his apparent haste, he had taken time out to get a bottle of whisky, a pitcher of water, and two glasses. He indicated a chair for Poco, who did not take it, took off his coat, poured two drinks, gave Poco one and sat down on the sagging, iron-framed bed.

"Didn't you get my letter?" Two-Way began.

Poco nodded.

"Then what's the trouble. Did you come all this way to tell me you wouldn't talk to me?"

"An accident," Poco said. "I happened to come this way."

"Because the army was chasing you. Is that it?"

Poco nodded.

"What happened?"

Poco said gently, "You ask a lot of questions."

"I've got to know," Two-Way said seriously. "If you're in a jam, it may spoil our plans. We can't have the army chasing you every time they get word you've been seen."

Poco thought a minute. "All right," he said. "I rode into Fort Benjamin last night and asked for feed for my horse. They gave it to me and put me up too. This morning when I was leaving I asked what it would cost. They wouldn't take any money. I made them take me to the commandant. He wouldn't take any money either. I don't take charity. I told him so. He said the army didn't either, and that he wouldn't take it. I gave it to him."

"How?"

"I rammed it down his throat."

"You—" Two-Way began and then his voice trailed off. He said, "You say you rammed it down his throat?"

"Yes."

Two-Way shook his head, staring at Poco. "There's no harm done, then, except they're sore. Is that all?"

"Just a little touchy."

Two-Way threw back his head and laughed loud, while Poco watched him, unsmiling. Then Two-Way raised his glass in mock toast, but there was admiration in his eyes. "Here's to your guts, Poco. God, but I'm glad there's only one of you."

He drank while Poco leaned against the wall and

watched him. Two-Way, now that he had Poco in a listening mood, was inclined to savor it and put off telling his story as long as he could, and Poco let him. He offered Poco a cigar and when Poco refused, lit one himself and sprawled against the head of the bed.

"Well, Poco," he began expansively, "I've got something. Something big. If it goes through, we'll drown in gravy. You won't need money again. You'll never even have to think of it. You can forget there is such a thing as money and just buy and do and say what you want."

"I do anyway," Poco said.

Two-Way looked at him levelly. "You do, don't you? Well, I don't. I want money. I need it. You could use some, couldn't you?"

Poco nodded.

Two-Way said gently, watching Poco, "Especially if it was money taken from Abe McCandless, huh?"

A tiny light of interest leaped into Poco's eyes. Two-Way noted it, and said, "He's a shrewd old cuss, Poco. You found that out, didn't you?"

Poco kept quiet.

"You've always wondered who fixed it up so that when you rode into Socorro after that big Wells Fargo holdup, you were arrested and identified as the robber." He paused and watched Poco's face. "Did you know that Abe McCandless was the only passenger on that stage, and that the driver and the guard were killed so they couldn't possibly have identified you?"

"I heard it," Poco said.

Two-Way tongued his cigar with relish, then said, "Well, Abe McCandless, besides owning a dozen ranches, a couple of towns, a pack of tough gunmen and three sheriffs, owns a mine." He took the cigar from his mouth. "It's up in the San Jons—way up in the San Jons. In fact, it's on top of the San Jons—right dead, smack on top of the highest peak in the San Jons."

"I heard you."

"Think what it means. Know anything about mining?"

"No."

"Neither do I. Only I know that gold is where you find it and you generally don't find it on top of a mountain range, because it washes down over a hundred miles of ground, is caught in some pockets, is found along creek beds and such. You know that."

Poco nodded. He was interested now.

Two-Way continued. "There's a dozen prospectors working that San Jon slope and they make good wages. But Abe McCandless is on top. Don't that tell you anything?"

"You mean the mother lode of that field is up there."

"That's just what I mean," Two-Way said emphatically. "I don't say I think it, or guess it, or just figured it out. I *know* it!"

"How?"

"Let me go back," Two-Way said. "Last summer Abe McCandless hired a dozen men and the best mining men money could buy. He had tons of grub and tools freighted up to timber line. Then he set a crew to cutting timber. His men spent all summer getting that grub and stuff—and firewood, mind you—up to that camp on the peak. They built their shacks and started in and they stayed there all winter. More than that, they worked all through the winter. Everyone around here laughed at them, but they laughed too soon." He pointed his cigar at Poco. "They found gold. They found a hell of a lot. Roughly, it's worth more than a quarter million dollars."

"That's a lot of money," Poco said gently. "I don't believe it. If they did, all of Christian City and the whole army would move up and stake claims."

"They don't know it."

"How do you?"

Two-Way grinned. "That's what I'm coming to. Some of it I've had to guess at. Some of it I know." He got up and went over to his coat and drew out a packet of papers which he tossed on the bed before he sat down again.

"A couple of weeks ago," he began slowly, "I had to leave Tombstone. I thought I'd come up here, so I took the stage. It was a long trip. Anyway, on the way we picked up a passenger, a young fella dressed in good clothes. I forget where we picked him up, but it was from another stage. Crossing the Mogollons, a storm hit us. It rained for three days. Nearly foundered the horses. When we got down out of the mountains we found that it was still raining. We couldn't make five miles a day, so when we came to the stage station at Apache Crossing, our driver gave up. We had to hole up in that single log shack and drink rotgut booze and smell the horses in the corral and play poker. Well, this man began to talk. I found out that he was a field agent for a big insurance company—a company that insures gold shipments and such against robbery, loss, fire, floods and such. He told me he was on his way to a job up in this country. He said all this when he was drunk. He—"

Poco raised a hand and Two-Way stopped talking. There was a thundering knock on the door of the next room, then silence. Poco lounged erect and strode across the room to a door which let on to the next room. He put his hand on the knob and opened the door. Turning to Two-Way still on the bed, he put a finger to his mouth, then fisted his hand and pretended to drink from it. Two-Way understood the pantomime. He reached over for the second glass, tucked it under his pillow and lay back, just as the same brand of knock racketed on his room door. Poco vanished into the next room and closed the door behind him.

The knock came again. Two-Way said thickly, "C'min."

The door opened and a blue-coated cavalry trooper, his black hat pushed back on his sweat-wet hair, stepped into the room. He wore sergeant's stripes on his sleeves. On his round red face was an expression of harried and weary truculence and hanging down from his hand was a six-gun. He wiped the sweat from his face and said, "I'm lookin' for a little fella with a red shirt."

Two-way waved with a broad and amiably drunken gesture and said thickly, "Fine. There's six of 'em sittin' on the foot of my bed. You c'n take two."

The sergeant glared at him, then at the foot of the bed,

then at him. "I mean it," the sergeant said.

"So do I. Take three."

The sergeant looked disgusted. "What's in there?" he asked pointing to the door Poco had just stepped through.

Two-way took a deep swig of whisky. "The school-teacher. She's got boils."

The sergeant growled in his throat and strode across the room. Two-Way watched with held breath as he flung the door open and strode into the room. Two-Way heard the outer door of the next room open and he was waiting for the sound of shots. Then he looked up and saw Poco standing just inside his room. It was still. Suddenly Poco streaked for the connecting door and vanished into the next room. The sergeant stuck his head in the corridor door.

"You're funny," he said wryly. "I hope this gent shoots you in the back. He's bad."

Two-Way stared at him soddenly. Then he drew his own gun and waved it at the sergeant. "S'm I," he said thickly. "I c'n shoot."

The sergeant pulled the door shut hurriedly and Poco stepped into the room and leaned against the wall.

"What about this insurance agent?" he said quietly.

Two-Way wiped the sweat from his forehead and gulped down a drink. Then he began again.

"Well, I remembered what he told me. When we got up to Silver City, I got hold of Tim Conaghan and arranged to—well, get his papers."

"Stick-up."

Two-Way nodded. "Tim bungled the job, but he got the papers. I read them." He pointed to the sheaf of papers still on the bed. "There they are. About the middle of winter, Shayne, this mine manager for McCandless, rigged up a pair of skis, put a man on them and shoved him down the mountain with word to the McCandless brothers that he had struck it. He said they had more than a quarter million dollars in gold there and that it would have to be got out in the spring as soon as the snow went. He told McCandless to keep it a secret, that if word got out in this country that they were bringing the stuff down, all the hard-cases above the border would gang up and take it. He's the one that told McCandless to write to this insurance outfit."

"Why?"

"So they could send two good tough men to take it out secretly."

Poco looked at him curiously. "How do you know all this?"

Again Two-Way pointed to the letters. "It's all in there. Shayne's letter and a copy was to be given to the two insurance men as a way to identify themselves when they appeared at the mine. Shayne told McCandless to hire the men but not to interview them, because it might arouse suspicion. So you're clear there. You won't have to see McCandless. All you do is take these papers—all of them will identify you as Jake Finger—up to Shayne, get the gold and disappear."

Poco said quickly, "You said two men."

Two-Way nodded and smiled crookedly. "There's the catch." He looked at Poco steadily now. "The other agent, as a matter of caution, was coming from El Paso. His stage was held up in the Tularosas by a gang and every passenger was killed. That happened last week."

Poco said gently, "Whose gang?"

Two-Way shrugged. "Whoever did it will know about that gold. They can't get it at the mine because a gang couldn't get up there. They'll send one man up there to pose as the insurance agent and he'll have the same papers you do. Once he gets off the mountain, he'll have a bunch waiting."

Two-Way said no more. He leaned back against the headboard and watched Poco who was scowling a little.

After a long moment, Two-Way said, "It's a tough proposition. I wouldn't blame you if you turned it down."

Poco's eyes focused fleetingly on him.

"Conaghan killed this Finger to get the papers. Is that it?" Poco said.

Two-Way nodded.

Poco said, "Is the snow gone enough so a man could reach the camp?"

"I've inquired around," Two-Way said, trying to stifle his growing excitement. "Some say it is, some say it isn't. You can try."

Poco lounged erect. "All right."

"You'll do it?" Two-Way asked quickly, and when Poco nodded once, he smiled broadly.

Putting his cigar down, he sat up and swung his feet off the bed. "Good. All that's left is the agreement." He looked seriously at Poco. "What do you say we make this a two-way proposition—fifty-fifty split?"

Poco almost smiled at this familiar phrase, the one that had earned Two-Way his name and lost many a man his life and fortune. He knew the arguments Two-Way would use to clinch his right to a half—arguments about brains, about furnishing the opportunity and papers and the means whereby all this would be made possible.

He only said quietly, "I'll take sixty. You take forty."

Two-Way stood up, protest on his face. "Why, dammit, Poco, that's robbery! Here I gave you the scheme, the papers, the—"

"I don't haggle," Poco said gently, flatly. "Take it or leave it, and do it now."

Two-Way's own frustration gagged him. He started to speak and then checked himself and sat down on the bed, glaring at Poco. "Now look here, Poco. I wrote—"

"What'll it be?" Poco cut in.

Two-Way glared at him in impotent fury. Then he laughed quietly, ruefully, grudgingly, shaking his head slowly. He raised his hands elbow high, palms up, and shrugged. "I'll have to take it, I guess. I called you in on this, though, because I knew you were one man I could trust, a man who would be fair and stick to his word. Maybe I made a mistake."

Poco regarded him a moment, then walked over to the bed and laid both hands on the footboard. "Maybe you did," he said flatly. "Do you think you did?"

Two-Way shook his head emphatically, his eyes uneasy.

Poco continued, "I'll tell you why you called me in here. Because you don't have the guts—never did have, never will have—to carry out a thing like this. You're a rat, Two-Way. With any guts, you'd be a real crook. But you've got a big wide, woolly yellow stripe down your back that a shirt won't cover. It grows into your hair and it covers your heels and it weighs just about what you do. And it won't wash off. Remember that."

Two-Way's face was flushed with anger, but he said no word. Poco smiled crookedly, and then he said in a pleasant voice, "I'll have a look at those papers."

CHAPTER THREE

IT WAS A TWO DAYS' RIDE from Christian City to the foothills of the San Jons, the first half of it through gaunt-ribbed, switchback canyons that wove their maze tilting to the San Jon tableland to the west. This gently rolling and grassy plateau, Poco remembered, was part of the Mc-Candless holdings, as were most of the unfenced and lush grazing lands in a half-dozen counties to the south. He recalled with a quiet and impassive bitterness that it was on just such a range as this, only farther south, that he had served his apprenticeship under Abe McCandless. He had been a youngster then, tough, eager to learn, and he had accepted the starvation wages, the endless work, the primitive living of that frowsy and unlovely home ranch without complaint.

He had been loyal then, caught in the fever of helping to build a cattle empire, and the twenty a month Abe paid him seemed a generous sum for which to fight and maverick and risk his life a dozen times a week. But the day a conscientious sheriff rode into the home ranch and was closeted with big Abe McCandless for several hours, Poco learned and digested a large slice of life.

The memory of it, undimmed by years, came back now. Stretched out under the lone cottonwood by the black-smith shop, on that day years ago, he was smoking contentedly when a hand told him McCandless wanted him. In the office he faced Abe and the sheriff, a slight, small-boned youngster tough beyond his years, a strange mixture of self-reliance and loyalty. Abe started the ball rolling by announcing that even a kid must pay for his mistakes, that the sheriff had positive evidence against him, and that he, Abe, proposed to harbor no murderers.

"Murderer?" Poco had echoed.

The sheriff said, "A nester over here on the Cuerva rim was killed yesterday. He must have put up a fight, because there were signs of a struggle, on horses and off. A TC iron was found nearby. You were seen over that way. McCandless said he gave orders to you to talk to this nester. How about it? Will you confess to me or to a judge or to your God?"

"He's yours, Sheriff," Big Abe said when Poco did not answer. "I hold no brief for a killer, young or old."

Those long still nights in jail, the hot quiet days, had shaped Poco more than he knew. He accepted the fact that it was a frameup, that McCandless had sacrificed him, a friendless orphan, as the least important cog in his vast machine that was strangling and digesting this country with the rapacious hunger of an octopus. It fed his fury until it burned like a still cold flame inside him. The jail couldn't hold him, and he escaped, but it was to turn his back on the country. Even then, he knew he could not fight Abe McCandless, but he never forgot.

In later years, when he had been hunted over a thousand trails, when men held their peace when he walked into a room, when his name had become at once a threat and a curse, he looked back on his days under McCandless with a kind of wry affection. They had opened his eyes, had made him realize that a man stands unutterably alone in this world, a hungry, sometimes cunning animal whose prey is his fellow man, because of his stupidity. But he had never forgotten. In a private citadel of his mind, there was that same boy's anger and hurt that he had felt facing Abe and the sheriff in the office. It was unchanged, untarnished, wicked. He knew some day he would have to kill Mc-

Candless, but he wanted to hurt him first, to make him crawl, beg for his life, to walk always in the shadow of death.

Nothing Two-Way Hornbeck had told him had fooled him. He knew Two-Way, the day they met to split up the gold, would have recruited a gang of hard-cases who would hunt him from border to border to retrieve his share, but he was unworried. A third of a lifetime spent with Two-Way's stripe had taught him only a contempt for them. He realized that Two-Way knew his honesty would bring him back to share the loot and be killed, but this honesty was the last thing Poco clung to in a world of fools and rogues. With pauper, sheriff, or cattle baron, Poco kept his word, and he had told Two-Way he would meet him and share the loot. He would.

And now he reflected that Two-Way had the makings of a great man, crooked or honest, because no detail had been too small for his cunning mind. Two-Way had even ridden this way and had carefully mapped out a route that would take him to the trail that led to the San Jons peaks. He ate at noon by a spring at the base of a tall rock outcrop that lined up with the scrub-oak thicket where he had camped last night under the deep scar of a burn on the side of the San Jons peaks.

By mid-afternoon he had picked up the freight trail and followed it. It was dim, some of it grassed over by the spring growth, but there was a telltale blaze of ax marks where the way had been cleared that made it plain as a highway. Crossing a jackpine *cienega* in late afternoon, Poco saw the tracks of a single horse in the mud. They were more than a day old, and going his way. That, he reflected, would be the man posing as Herb Shelton, the other insurance agent who had been downed on the Tularosa stage. Who would it be? A man with brains enough to accept Poco as a partner until they got the gold down from the peaks, a man that would call him Jake Finger and ask after his days on the trail and engage in small talk of mutual friends while Shayne looked on and suspected nothing? Or would it be a fool, who would try to

give him away as an impostor? Poco smiled at this; he
liked a bluff, liked to run one, liked to see other people
run them and work them.

When dusk fell he was a little short of timber line, and
he made his camp in the V of two recent windfalls, and
built a fire. It was cold and by the time his horse was staked
out and some wood gathered, darkness was closing down.
He ate and rolled into his blankets.

By noon of the next day he was high in the boulder
fields above timber line with a steady frost-laden wind riding off the peaks towards him. There was snow here on
the north side of rocks and as he threaded his way higher,
spotting an occasional track of the other man's horse,
these spots of snow increased.

He looked ahead and to the right where the bulk of
Monarch peak seemed to rise sheer to the blue above.

Here, on the shoulder of Monarch, was where the trail
proper began, and he spent some time casting around
the marble slabs of this gray and silent desert for it. Picking up the tracks of a horse on the snow blanket, he got
the direction, followed it closer to the peak and finally
saw where the trail began its ascent.

It had been built on the south side of the peak to get
the sun, and immediately it began to lift. He rode as far
as he could on its narrow and tortuous shelf until he began to feel a crawling fear when he looked below him.
Rounding the shoulder of it now, he came to snow. The
man before him had broken a kind of trail and Poco led
his sorrel through it. In some places the trail was steep,
slippery, with a wall of snow on one side, a sheer drop to
the gray floor of the boulder fields below. It tried to stay
away from the north face, and mainly succeeded, but
where the snows had melted on the south face, it was
more treacherous. Shored up in some spots, it had been
almost washed away by the melting snows, and in these
places Poco felt trapped as he had never felt before. His
sorrel could never turn around here. They must go forward. Under his heavy windbreaker, he was wet with
sweat. The sorrel climbed patiently, more confident than

its master.

All through that afternoon, Poco kept his eyes glued to the trail. The flanking shoulder of the peak leveled off somewhat higher up, but as if to offset this advantage, the trail became narrower. His breath came short and labored in the thin air, and the frosty mountain gusts seemed bent on tearing him away from the wall.

Now he could see where the trail had been shoveled clear of the snow, and he guessed that these people on top, expecting their messengers, had worked down from the top with shovels. The trail almost circled the peak now with steeper and steeper switchbacks.

And then, when he was on the south face, he saw the trail widen in front of him. He looked up. Ahead there seemed to be a cleared space. And then he rounded the shoulder of rock ahead and he was there.

A great wide shelf had been blasted out of the mountain, while beyond it, scarcely a thousand feet higher, was the flattened top of the peak. On this tight triangular shelf there were five tar-papered shacks, the shaft house, a tool shed and mill house.

All this Poco saw in a brief glance while his sorrel whickered, then he pulled his gaze down to the cluster of silent people facing him and he noticed that more than one shotgun was leveled at him as he dismounted.

But of all these people, Poco had eyes for only one man. There, standing a half-head taller than any man in the crowd, an amused half-smile on his lean and sleepy face, stood Espey Cardowan, killer gunman, exiled Texan, shrewdest and most merciless of all those hounded men whose pictures were in every sheriff's office in the west.

He was wearing a borrowed Mackinaw which hid the twin guns sagging at his hips and he had his hands rammed deep into the pockets.

Poco looked at him a long moment, and then his face broke into a careless smile. "Hello, Herb," he said quietly, and he watched Cardowan.

"Howdy, Jake," Cardowan drawled in a soft and gentle voice that was lazy with good humor. His face went mostly to thin jaw, so that it gave him a look of keenness which was not false. In his gray-blue eyes, little flecks of brown played, and his smile was full, slow, pleasant, because his fine teeth flashed sharply against the dusky smoky tan of his face. But under the pleasant shell of the man, there was an alertness, a rapaciousness that lurked in his eyes, his mouth sometimes. He turned now to the man beside him and said, "There's my partner, Shayne. Jake Finger."

Shayne handed his shotgun to the man next him, saying, "It's all right, boys," and stepped over to Poco, holding out his hand in welcome. He was not a tall man, neither burly nor slight, and his face was rugged and yet sensitive, almost intellectual. His gray hair was closecut, his eyes keen and friendly, and his speech had a warmth in it. Somehow he seemed out of place in the soiled breeches and Mackinaw and the scuffed lace-boots.

"Welcome, Finger. We were getting a little worried. Have any trouble?"

Poco took the hand and said carelessly, "Ran into a lot of rain in the Mogollons. Held me up a couple of days."

Shayne nodded. He sensed the quiet, hard way of this little man, and he smiled. "Shelton told me I might be surprised by his partner, but he wouldn't say why. I think I am."

Poco looked up at Cardowan with a glance that paid him a measure of shrewd tribute. He said, "Herb still can't understand that a good little man is better than a good big man. He thinks other people can't."

Shayne laughed along with Cardowan. Then Shayne turned to a group who stood listening.

"Finger," he said, taking Poco's arm, "I want you to meet my daughter, Kate."

From out of the group of men, a girl stepped, in boots and a Mackinaw. She was dressed so like the men that Poco had missed her. And now, looking at her he wondered how he had, for she was hatless, and her hair was ash-white, blond beyond blond, and was thick and windblown and so finespun that it seemed unreal. Poco first saw this, and then his glance went to her face

while he automatically took off his hat, and accepted the
hand she held out.

He thought, looking at her face, that he had never seen
one so clean and untroubled. It held that serenity which
is more than beauty, though her lips were full and wide,
and her eyes of the same haunting blue as her father's.
But there was an eagerness in them, part humor, part
friendliness, that made Poco feel soiled and humble as he
touched her hand. The rough men's clothes she was wearing could not hide the grace of her body. Her skin was a
smooth gold a little darker than her hair, and Poco had
only one word for her beauty, and it was a word that he
had given to two horses in his whole life because no other
word caught their fineness quite so well. It was "clean."

"Hello," was all she said, but the one word, spoken in
a low voice, carried more than a speech of welcome.

Shayne said, "You're wondering what a girl is doing
up here?" He put an arm around her and looked at her
fondly. "Well, she wouldn't stay below. She's been here
all winter and she'll probably corner you and ask what a
tree looks like." He glanced at Cardowan, who had walked
up to stand beside Poco. "She's already asked Shelton if
it's true there won't be any summer this year."

Kate laughed and put an arm around her father.

"Don't you believe it. I'm going to stay up here when
the rest move down."

Poco stood tongue-tied, still-faced, watching her, nodding instead of speaking.

Shayne said to Kate, "Finger's hungry, darling. And
it isn't far from suppertime. Go tell cook to hustle it."

When she was gone, Shayne turned to Poco. "What do
you think of our set-up, Finger?" He pointed to the four
shacks. "That end one is yours and Shelton's. The second
is where Kate and I live. The third, that big one, is the
men's bunkhouse and the fourth the cookshack and mess
hall. Beyond the shacks there are the shaft house and the
mill." He pointed off to the biggest building hanging on
the very lip of the shelf to the east. It, like the others, was
snow covered. "That's our warehouse and stable for the

four horses. Come along and we'll feed your horse."

Cardowan, as the three walked over to the warehouse, said so Shayne could hear, "Any trouble, Jake?"

"Not a bit," Poco said easily. "How about you?"

Cardowan smiled a little. "Had a little scare in the Tularosas. A bunch fired on the stage, but we fought them off."

Poco looked at him and nodded. "I heard something about that. You ought to stick to a saddle. It's safe."

"I will from now on," Cardowan drawled.

When the sorrel was unsaddled, watered, fed and rubbed down, Shayne said, "Take your duffle over to the shack, Finger. I'll see you both at supper."

Out in the yard, Poco stopped and looked around him. It was the look he had been saving ever since he had started the climb that morning. To the south and below he could see nothing but the endless crooked spine of the San Jons, a twisting green serpent whose smashed and tortured backbone was thrust grayly up above the skin. It stretched sprawling and vast and still and indescribable to where sight failed. To the east, he could see the shadow of the mountains crawling over the low foothills as the sun set. Beyond that was only space, blurred at the bottom where the hundreds of miles of green grass floor tipped into canyons of sunbeaten rock. Far lower and beyond he could see the fawn of sagebrush flats that swelled and sunk until they merged into the blue wash that rimmed the desert and all the horizon. To the west there was only the brass ball of the sun that he could not look at and that was gilding the face of the peak above with a hard glare of gold.

He looked at it all and some corner of his mind understood it, but he did not feel humble. He beheld it all with a quiet arrogance that conceded it was big, and then he turned and walked to the shack where the long figure of Cardowan was framed in the door. He disappeared as Poco approached. Poco entered and closed the door. The lamp on the table at the end of the room between the two bunks was lighted and Cardowan leaned against the table, the light from below shadowing the lines of his face.

"Welcome, Poco," he drawled, and he laughed, making no sound.

Poco smiled musingly, his hands behind him. "Hello, Joker. You always come back for more, don't you?"

Cardowan was still smiling. "You've won the other times, Poco. This time you won't."

"No?"

"No. This is the last time we meet," Cardowan said lazily, watching him with those gray eyes that were shallow as rain and hard as a bird's.

Poco looked around the room with mild interest, and then his gaze settled on Cardowan and it was as if he had just recalled that he wasn't alone. "You wouldn't be that lucky, Joker," he drawled arrogantly.

Cardowan's face flushed a little, but the smile was fixed, triumphant. He said, "You've stuck your nose in my business just once too often, Poco. That time you held my bunch up after we stuck up the Indian agency, I didn't mind so much."

"Of course not," Poco said carelessly. "Money's easy to get. Especially when somebody else gets it for you."

Cardowan ignored this, but the smile was fading. "I even didn't mind it much when you packed that stage on the Whitewater run with a bunch of your own gunnies because you heard I'd raid it."

Poco laughed with the memory of it. "How many men did you lose that time? We counted ten before you ran."

Cardowan ignored this, too, but the smile was gone. "You won all those, Poco, and a lot more, but this time you won't. You're trapped. My men let you through below. They'll be waiting when we come down."

Poco yawned, and it was like a cat's yawn: clean, full, quick, anything but sleepy. It might have been from boredom—or so Cardowan thought.

He drawled jeeringly, "Still cocky, huh?"

Poco stared at him blankly, then walked over to a bunk, unbuckling his shellbelts and gunbelt on the way. He threw them all on the bed, then rolled up his sleeves and went to the frame washstand, which held a pitcher of water and a basin.

"Did you know it would be me?" Cardowan asked curiously, after a silence, watching him.

Poco only nodded and began to soap his hands.

Cardowan said, "How?"

Poco cast about for a plausible lie and found none, so he said, "There's only one killer riding this country that would shoot every passenger on a stage just to see the others squirm. Who would it be but you?"

"Thanks," Cardowan said flatly. "And knowing that, you came up anyway."

Poco said, "Do you run from a rattlesnake?" and began to wash.

For a while the only sound in the room was the slick whisper of him lathering his face.

Then Cardowan said, "No, I kill it."

Poco looked up, his face soapy, and opened an eye. "You catch on quick."

Cardowan lounged off the table and in one motion had pulled his gun and cocked it and pointed it dead level at Poco's body. Poco looked up at it and went back to his washing and when he had his face rinsed and wiped and his eyes open again, the gun was still pointing at him.

"Maybe I better settle this now," Cardowan said. "If that's the turn, I can call it first. I could kill you and tell Shayne you're Poco St. Vrain. He's heard of you. Everybody has."

Poco said patiently, "The time for that is past, Joker. You should have done that the second you saw me. If you do it now, figure it out for yourself."

Cardowan did not put up his gun. He spoke now in a flat voice, a voice that went beyond earnest passion. "Listen, you. Every time we've tangled, you've come out on top." He leaned forward now and his gun sagged. "But you're crowding your luck, Poco. You can't turn to Shayne. You can't kill me for the same reason I can't kill you. We'll get that gold and we'll go down the mountain and you'll walk into thirty guns down there." He watched Poco a still second, then he leaned back and holstered his gun. "You can't crowd me into making a play before Shayne. You couldn't kill me on a fair play even if you did. I won't waste time talking about it."

Poco said with superb indifference, "That's right. You've wasted enough already."

Cardowan lounged off the table and confronted him. Little lines of muscle bulged on his lean jaw. "Some day," he began in a thick voice, "some day soon, I'm going to slit you below the bottom rib and reach in and tear your heart out! You'll watch it, too!"

Poco said, "Tsk, tsk," and reprovingly began to roll down his sleeves.

A knock came on the door and someone outside said, "Come and get it," and then walked away.

Poco grinned broadly now. "Think you can eat, Joker?"

Cardowan had never ceased looking at Poco. Now he said, "If I thought you had a pack of hard-cases down there waiting too, I'd kill you now."

Poco laughed and opened the door. "I'll tell you a little story about that tonight."

Together they walked over to the mess shack. Inside, Shayne and Kate were waiting, and Poco was introduced to the dozen men who had worked under Shayne the long winter through. Then they seated themselves, Shayne at the head of the table, Kate next to Cardowan on one side of Shayne, Poco on the other. It was a festive occasion, celebrating the successful termination of a year's work, and tonight when Poco and Cardowan signed the insurance papers, the task of guarding and preserving the vast fortune in gold would be transferred to their shoulders. Poco didn't wonder that the men felt as if a burden had been lifted from them.

He glanced at Cardowan, and saw hate in his eyes.

Shayne, naturally enough, could not wait to hear the details of the shipment which the insurance company had worked out, but Poco, wary, parried his every attempt.

"You'll meet more of your men down below somewhere, of course?" Shayne asked.

Poco shook his head. "I couldn't tell you if we were,

Shayne. That's company business."

Shayne nodded. "Naturally, but I'm interested. So will McCandless be, my owner."

Poco looked over at the sullen Cardowan, and said politely, "You tell him, Herb."

Cardowan shot a glance of quiet fury at Poco, but his face was as polite, as impassive as ever. "Jake does all the talking for the company, Shayne."

Poco nodded in mock gravity. He explained to Shayne, "I can't tell you, and here's why. We underwrite this shipment. When it leaves here, it's our business to guard it till it gets to its destination. All right, what if you took three or four men down the trail tonight, hid them, and waited till we came along with the gold. What if McCandless told you to. You'd stick us up, maybe kill us, and take the gold. The company would have to pay McCandless the amount that was stolen, and still McCandless would have the gold." He shrugged. "It's been tried. We're careful."

Shayne laughed easily and admitted the possibility.

Kate said, "You say it's been done? I would think the insurance company would hunt those men down if it took them years."

Poco nodded politely, when Cardowan cut in with his easy, soothing drawl. "You'd be surprised how slippery some of those crooks are, ma'am. You take one man that's been pretty famous down in our part of the country." He looked at Poco. "His name's Poco St. Vrain, a little short ranny, about Jake's size there. He's a rat, he'd doublecross his friends and his men, and he's done it time and again. He's wanted by every sheriff west of the Pecos. He's hired out time and again to these crooked mining men to steal their stuff for them after it's been insured."

He had been talking to Kate, but now he looked across at Poco. "But his time's near up, ma'am. We'll get him." He smiled cunningly now. "This company I work for, ma'am, never forgets. And when we get him"—he snapped his fingers swiftly—"there won't be any trial, ma'am."

Kate said slowly, "You mean you'd kill him—right there, without giving him justice?"

"He's killed a dozen men, miss, shot them in the back, tortured them, broken them, doublecrossed them too. He's hated by outlaws as much as he is by the law."

Poco wiped his mouth and shoved his plate away. "But he's a queer one, Miss Kate," he began gently. "First thing in his favor is, he's got brains. The run-of-the-mill outlaw down there is usually a Texan chased across the line. He's a killer, right enough, but he hasn't brains. Now this St. Vrain, I remember one story about him that just shows you." He looked up briefly at Cardowan. "There's a dumb ranny of a Texas outlaw down in our country by name of Espey Cardowan. Ever heard of him?"

"I have," Kate said quickly. "I've heard of St. Vrain, too. Go on."

"Well, this Cardowan made the mistake of cold-decking St. Vrain in a card game one night below the border, and then pulling out of the game behind the guns of his own men. St. Vrain didn't forget that. He never forgets anything. Word came to him that a troop of soldiers who'd been campaigning against the Apaches for three months would be paid off in the town of White Bend. St. Vrain knew that meant money in the town, and a lot of it. He figured the word would get to Cardowan too, because Cardowan was riding that country with his bunch."

"Why was that so important?" Kate asked.

"Why, as soon as the troops cleared out Cardowan would clean the White Bend Bank."

Kate nodded understandingly.

"Well, a bunch of rangers had been working on this same Apache hunt and they teamed with the army now and then. They were at a town about fifteen miles away that night. Seven Troughs." He looked at Cardowan. "Ever hear of it, Herb?"

Cardowan nodded curtly.

"The army paid off on Saturday and left Sunday. The minute they'd left town, Cardowan's gang drifted in and kind of took over the town, waiting for Monday when the bank's doors would be open. St. Vrain had a man there in town. As soon as he saw Cardowan's bunch drift in, the man got word to St. Vrain. St. Vrain forged a note from the captain of the troopers asking the rangers to drift over to White Bend and stay there till further notice. St. Vrain took the note himself, posing as a civilian scout."

"What happened?" Shayne asked.

Poco smiled slowly. "Why, just after sunrise the rangers came pounding into White Bend and camped at the only hotel in town. When the bank opened that morning there was six of them sitting on the hotel porch making jokes with the fellow that swept out the bank across the street."

Before Poco's last word had died, the table was laughing uproariously, Kate and Shayne along with the men.

The meal broke up and then Cardowan and Poco were called into Shayne's place, which was double locked and shuttered. There Poco showed his credentials, had them accepted, and then the business of weighing the gold got under way. Shayne had it stored in an iron-bound chest which was double locked and bolted to the floor under the table. When the table was moved, the scales placed on the table, the chest was opened. Poco saw it was almost filled with uniform bricks of gold, a little smaller than a building brick.

Shayne pointed to it and said, "Ever see so much?"

Poco, sitting on the edge of the bunk, looked at it carelessly. "Lots of times." He turned his head to Cardowan, who was staring at it with eyes wide and shiny with greed. "Have you, Herb?"

Cardowan shook his head. "That's the most I ever saw," he drawled.

There was an inordinate amount of time spent in weighing the gold bricks, counting them and in signing papers. Poco had been coached by Two-Way in the preparing of the papers, so that he ran through them with a speed and knowledge that surprised Cardowan. When finally Shayne wrote his signature to it, he sighed and looked up at Kate, who was curled up on the other bunk watching the procedure.

"There. The biggest job in my life is done." He smiled at Poco and Cardowan. "You'll sleep with this stuff tonight. I never want to see it again."

Poco nodded, rolling his cigarette.

"You'll have to pack this stuff out," Shayne continued. "Kate has made up some canvas sacks you can pack it in so it'll ride on the mules. We'll help you put it away if you give the word."

"I reckon we can," Poco said. "We've nothing to do tonight but get this stuff ready. Give us the sacks and we'll take it over to our shack."

He and Cardowan, with the help of two men, unbolted the chest and moved it over to their cabin. They set it between the two bunks, dismissed the men and then they both sat down facing each other. Cardowan's gaze kept resting on the chest, as if he could not believe what it contained. Poco watched him with still, amused aloofness.

Finally he said, "Don't worry, Joker. I'll pay you wages if you'll help me pack the stuff in those sacks."

Cardowan said blankly, "Pay me wages?"

"Sure, it'll be mine. I wouldn't want you to work all night for nothing."

Cardowan cursed him with flawless, passionate oaths, and Poco only smiled. But soon they were at work with the gold bricks, packing them a dozen to the sack, wrapping the sacks in the tarp and packing them in the *aparejos*. When the job was finally finished and the sacks stored, they faced each other across the empty chest.

Cardowan pulled out the makings and Poco noticed that his fingers were trembling as he rolled his cigarette. Poco said nothing.

Suddenly Cardowan blurted out, "Let's settle this now. We've got to go down that trail single file. Who'll go first?"

Poco said, "Why worry about that?"

Cardowan dropped his cigarette, cursing, and said, "Do you think I'd let you behind me with a gun?"

Poco lay back against the wall and pulled his feet up on the edge of the bunk. "There won't be any guns, Joker. Guns, knives, ropes, they'll all be in those mule packs."

Cardowan considered this a long time, staring at Poco,

calculating the advantages of this compromise. Presently he said, "You'll walk into my men without your guns, huh? Even you haven't that much guts, Poco."

"What makes you think I'll walk into your men?"

Cardowan smiled narrowly. "You can't fly off this peak."

"You'd be surprised what I can do, Joker. That's my headache. The guns will be in the mule packs."

"But who'll go first?"

Poco shrugged. "Why not cut cards?"

Cardowan nodded and got up to search for a pack of cards. He looked in the table drawer and immediately drew out a deck which he handed to Poco. Poco ruffled them, gave them back. Cardowan did the same. The deck was split, and each man cut his half four times, then it was merged, cut once by mutual agreement and rested, neat and orderly under the circle of lamplight.

"Low man leads off on the trail. If we tie, we discount the suit and draw again. Suit you?" When Cardowan nodded, Poco said. "Go ahead."

Cardowan turned up a jack. He sat back and watched Poco for any mismove as Poco turned up a seven.

Cardowan's face broke into a relieved smile. "The trap's shut, Poco. How does it feel?"

Poco yawned and rose. "Don't hide any of that stuff in your boots, Joker. We'll watch each other dress tomorrow morning."

CHAPTER FOUR

HE STEPPED OUT into the night, and immediately felt the cool steady wind pressing against him. There was a coming moon, and high above, it was lost and cold and thin in the vault of the sky. Poco strolled over to the edge of the cleared space and looked down on the slumbering San Jons washed with a sparse light. His thoughts were beating around in his skull like a bird in a cage. For he was trapped. He didn't have any men waiting below to meet him. Even if he made that drawling Texas killer inside believe he had, it wouldn't do any good. Cardowan had guts. He'd match his men against Poco's, and himself against Poco, and he'd gamble, because the odds were in his favor. Poco cursed soundlessly. He had thought of all this, of the possibility that the man who would pose as Herb Shelton would have his bunch waiting below. But he had trusted to his luck and his ingenuity and his reputation, because he was fighting for a fortune and because always in the back of his mind was the desire to even the score with McCandless.

But he had blundered. Any other crook but Espey Cardowan could have been bluffed, scared, bought off. But in these years that he had been riding the dark trails, he had gone out of his way to hurt Cardowan, because he hated him for his needless cruelty and for a blood lust that had long since won the respect of the Apaches. And Cardowan neither forgave nor forgot.

He cursed himself again. He could go back into the shack now, slug and tie Cardowan, fill a pack sack with all the gold he could carry and sneak down the trail tonight. But even the thought of that trail at night made his stomach ball up. Besides, Cardowan wouldn't be fool enough to leave the trail below unguarded.

Thinking thus, he heard a sound behind him, and at the same time Kate Shayne's voice said, "Hello."

Poco whirled, startled, and then remembered himself. "Hello," he answered.

She was beside him now, and he noticed for the first time that she was shorter than he. Looking out over the moon-washed mountains, she said, "They aren't near as grand in full moonlight."

Poco said, "No."

She looked at him now. "Does it make you not want to ever talk again?"

Poco glanced at her obliquely and said, "No. People can do that to me."

She caught his glance and regarded him calmly for a full moment. "I'll go," she said.

Poco said nothing. She turned away, walked a few steps,

then wheeled and came back. "I'm hanged if I will!" she said in a low angry voice. "You can be as rude as you want. You won't drive me off."

Surprised now, Poco observed her, but there was not one jot of apology in his tone when he said, "I didn't mean you."

"You mean everybody," Kate said flatly. "I've been watching you ever since you came up here with your sneering face and that smile that seems to hurt you. You don't trust or like anybody except yourself, do you?"

Poco turned this over in his mind and said, surprisingly. "That's right. Who else would I?"

"Not Shelton, certainly. You don't like him. I could tell that."

Poco smothered a start. "He's all right."

"Next to you," Kate said. "He falls in the class everybody else is in. To be tolerated, not liked."

Poco just looked at the mountains and said nothing and the silence dragged. Finally Kate said, "I'm sorry I said that. It was none of my business. I hardly know you." She laughed. "You see, I expected someone different. It's been lonely here."

Poco said sardonically without looking at her, "Go on. It sounds like we're married."

Instead of getting angry, Kate did not speak, and Poco looked at her, puzzled.

Kate said, "What has happened to you?"

"Nothing." Poco still regarded her with his insolent stare. "What's happened to you? I thought I was minding my own business until you came along."

Kate laughed uneasily. "Nothing, I guess. Only I've been up here all winter, seeing the same faces, getting to know these men. I like them. And then you two come up from below. You've been with people, lots of people, and you moved around through lots of country. But Shelton is close-mouthed, never speaks unless to answer a question. And you."

"What about me?"

"I've watched you. You weren't glad to see your friend,

Shelton. You build up a wall of reserve every time I try to talk to you. Don't you see, can't you understand that I'm eager to hear things, to talk, to hear about the world? I've been dead, you might say, for a year. I'm bursting with curiosity, and you treat me like—like a dance-hall girl." Her voice trailed off in bewilderment.

"Maybe you're sick," Poco said dryly.

"I don't think so," Kate answered gravely. "I'm just a human being that likes laughter and fun and people my own age and—and consideration." She paused. "I wonder. Is the whole world getting like this? Surly and unlikeable?"

"It always has been," Poco said.

"Have you ever stopped to think that people like you on first sight?" Kate asked. "You could make friends, lots of them, if you weren't like a porcupine."

"I've got a job, enough money, what it takes to live," Poco replied. "What else do I need?"

"What do you?" Kate echoed. "I know what I need. If people don't like me, I'm unhappy. I need love and—and respect, and affection and someone to lean on."

"You're a woman."

"Dad does too. He pays it back, though. He helps people, tries to be kind and tolerant and just. He's kept these men in harmony all winter. He saw what a temptation it was for them to be mining a fortune every week and only drawing wages for it, just because somebody else had luck. Do you know what he did?"

"No."

"He fought for a thousand dollar bonus for every man. Before the snow closed in last fall, he got it for them from Abe McCandless. These men would die for him now."

Poco said, "Give one of them a gun, enough shells, a key to your door, the keys to the chest, and a chance to make a getaway, then see. They might die for him if he shot them. That's all."

Kate did not move, did not say anything, but Poco had the feeling that he was being reproved, and that he should not have said what he did.

"I don't understand how you've worked for this company as long as you have," Kate said at last, and there was no reproof in her voice. "People don't like your kind around them."

"I'm tough," Poco said tonelessly. "I earn my pay. I can fight, I've got brains, I've got guts."

"Isn't that what you said about St. Vrain tonight?" Kate asked. When Poco only shifted uncomfortably, she continued. "I think you admire him."

"I do."

"An outlaw?"

"That's chance," Poco said carelessly. "If he'd been treated with kindness and decency and—"

"Toleration," Kate put in. "All those things you were ridiculing a minute ago. If he'd had all that when he needed it, he'd have been a fine, strong, silent law-abiding man like you. Is that it?"

She turned and paused long enough to say, "Maybe so. But if he turned out like you, perhaps he's better off where he is. Good night."

Poco felt his face hot as he bid her good night. When she was gone, his lip lifted in a soundless oath. A preacher —a woman preacher who looked like an angel and talked like a pious circuit rider. She'd been babied all her life, given things, and what wasn't given to her she could get with a little smart flirting or teasing. What did she know about men, about a man that was thrown on his own when he was a kid, framed when he was seventeen, hunted and hounded until he was driven into shooting his way to a goal? But underneath all this self-justification, Poco sensed a grain of truth in what she said. Sternly he shut it from his mind, all of it. He had more important things to worry about than a girl who called him names.

He was cold now, and he strolled back to the shack and entered it. Cardowan was ready to go to bed.

"That's a good-looking gal," he said slyly. "Do yourself any good?"

Something bright and hot flamed up in Poco and he strode across the room and pulled Cardowan off the bed.

"You cheap killer slob!" he said thickly. "Talk of her again and I'll kill you now and the gold be damned!"

Cardowan shrunk away. In all his dealings with Poco St. Vrain, he had always beheld a cool, insolent, nerveless piece of machinery who seemed not to have a temper. Now he was looking at a wild man, strangling with rage.

He said, "Take it easy, Poco. Hell, I didn't say anything."

"Don't," Poco said, and released him. Cardowan fell back on the bed, and watched Poco undress with a wondering gaze. Finally he pulled himself together.

"We better put a gun by us," he drawled. "Some of these wild miners might think we looked easy. That trail isn't guarded at this end."

"All right, Joker," Poco said easily. His temper was gone. He drew his gun and laid it on the table where he could reach it by raising his hand. The Texan did the same. Cardowan was in his bunk. Poco leaned over to blow out the light when he saw Cardowan's gun. "Ever walk down a street without one of those things?" he asked.

Cardowan said dryly, "Have I ever gone a year without eating?"

Poco blew the light. In bed, he lay with open eyes thinking about tomorrow. He was trapped, sure as day followed night. He tried to think of a way out, but he found the image of Kate Shayne, her serene face bathed in the pale moonlight, crowding out all other thoughts. Why had he lost his temper with Cardowan over a remark that usually he would have grinned at? Was he getting soft? He didn't know, lying there with his hands over his head. He went to sleep that way, with Cardowan's uneasy breathing a little louder than the wind at the cabin corners.

CHAPTER FIVE

THEY WATCHED EACH OTHER dress the next morning. Poco searched Cardowan for hideouts and then Cardowan searched him. They were both sobered by the thought that their truce had only an hour or so to run, and when they left this camp, it would be the old dog-eat-dog game.

Breakfast was noisy. That day, after Poco and Cardowan left, the men would start to break camp. It was an event for them. Everyone except Kate and Poco seemed in high spirits. She ate her breakfast almost in silence, and did not look at Poco once, while he talked with Shayne just enough so as not to arouse any suspicion.

After breakfast, preparations got under way. Two mules were brought out. The two big *aparejos* were filled with the sacks roped on to the mules, while Poco's and Cardowan's horses were being saddled. The sun did not warm this height; a steady cold breeze whipped through camp.

When everything was ready, Shayne said, "Who'll lead off?"

"Jake will," Cardowan drawled quickly. "He's in a hurry to get down."

Shayne shook hands with them and bid them luck. Kate, standing by her father, said good-by to Cardowan and then turned to Poco. He raised his hat.

"Good-by, Miss."

"Good-by. Good luck," she said quietly, and Poco saw something in her eyes that was cold, almost hostile.

He turned now and took the trail, the two pack mules behind his sorrel, Cardowan's roan behind them.

When Poco was ten feet down the trail a cold panic seized him. This was the last step. He had to go on now, and he knew what was waiting for him below. They crept around the mountain in cautious descent, and Poco found all thoughts of what was waiting below had vanished. Again it was hard to breathe, again he felt his stomach go tight and coil as he glimpsed the piled snow that blanketed the great gorges and canyons the trail hovered over.

He looked back once, and Cardowan, seeing him, smiled.

"Want to go back, Poco?" Cardowan called. Poco only grinned, a little sickly, and turned around.

The descent was slow and cautious. When they had passed the places on the trail that had washed out, Poco felt a great relief flood over him. These mules were sure-footed and more cautious than a horse.

On the north face, overlooking a deep gorge, the trail widened. Poco halted. "Let's have a smoke," he called.

Cardowan nodded. "I'll stay here, Poco," he said, smiling meaningly.

They both built smokes, and Poco squatted on his heels in front of his sorrel. Presently Cardowan called, "Throw me a match."

Poco threw one, but it was yanked out over the cliff by the wind. He tried another. The same thing happened.

Cursing, Cardowan flattened himself against the mountainside and edged past both the mules until he was behind Poco's sorrel. Poco, standing now, watched him stop there.

"Try it again," Cardowan said.

Poco smiled narrowly. "You couldn't be afraid to come up here, could you, Joker?"

"I could be, but I'm not. I've got more sense," Cardowan drawled easily. "Why risk a sure thing? You got another match?"

Poco threw him some, and now they hunkered on their haunches, eight feet of trail between them, and smoked. Poco was stalling, hoping against hope something would turn up to suggest a way of escape. The trail was impossible, and even the thought of a leap off the sheer drop made him almost sick. With a savage irony, he thought of what an ignominious death he faced. He had a choice of a broken back or being shot down by a cheap killer.

The wind was swooping down from the peaks, pressing him against the wall. A strong gust whipped the sorrel's trailing reins almost out straight, then it died.

Poco rose, Cardowan a second behind him.

"Let's go," Poco said.

Cardowan said nothing, watching him. Poco reached under his sorrel's neck to sweep in the reins which were trailing on the off side, hanging over the trail edge.

And in that moment, Cardowan struck the three matches he had in his hand on the rock, and when they were mounting into full flare, he jabbed them into the sorrel's rump, at the same time hugging the wall.

The sorrel yanked his head up, exploded ahead, smashing into Poco, a squeal welling in its throat.

Poco made one frantic grab as he felt himself off balance, and then the sorrel rocketed by him, butting him with a terrific impact. And in that one brief half-second of cold horror in which he clawed at the air, he heard Cardowan's laugh rise on the wind.

And then he was over, the trail whipping up out of sight, the sky and mountains wheeling crazily past his vision, his muscles locking in horror, his chest constricted and strangling him. There was a crazy kaleidoscope of snow and sky and rock and then something smashed all the wind out of him and he felt the cold slap of snow, and still he was falling, rolling now, aimless, helpless and his great retching gasps for air were choked off by snow in his mouth. All the flailing of his arms, the clawing of his hands, gathered only icy handfuls of snow as he turned over and over, while the very core of his life and being was slammed out of him by these blows that followed each other in lightning succession. He was drowning, fighting instinctively, when he felt a vast and almost painless shock on his head and blackness seemed to finish the work of strangulation in a showering pinwheel of light.

When he came to, it was only to open his eyes and let flinty flakes of snow into them. He tried to move and found that if he fought the pain enough, he could. In a wild and panicky surge, he flung the snow away from him and saw the cold sky above. He was almost buried in a deep drift, and his hands were locked into bloody and unfeeling claws. The snow was spotted with scarlet smears. He could see that much as he tried to focus his eyes.

The sun was past its zenith, behind the mountain. He struggled unsteadily to his feet, the snow waist deep about him. He smeared handfuls of snow on his face, and the bite of its cold cleared his head.

Then he looked around him. He was in the bottom of a deep gorge that was choking with snow. Looking up, he saw the walls rise sheer to the heavens. Turning, he could see part of the course his fall had taken, great jagged scars in the snow forty feet apart. Thirty feet above him, the scar dug deep and coursed in a long sweeping gully that ended where he was standing.

He looked at it, wondering how far he had fallen, when he saw, perhaps a dozen yards to the right of the scars his fall had made in the snow, still bigger scars.

And then he understood. His sorrel had gone over too. He looked across the floor of the gorge, which rose to a high snowbank forty yards to his left. He could see nothing except the unbroken white of its surface, but he knew the horse was there.

And now he began to stamp a trail in the snow in that direction, packing it with his feet, breaking down the crust, and in ten minutes he was exhausted. But for an hour he worked doggedly and as he neared the snowbank, he saw where it was disturbed. Closer now, he could see a dark spot of hide. When he reached it he saw the sorrel was buried deep in the snow. Dully, he scraped away the loose drift around the head until it was clear. One glance told him the sorrel was dead, its neck broken.

It was still warm, and he sat down on its side and put his head in his hands. Something hurt in his head, and the hand came away bloody.

For a while he sat there staring, a hot and furious bitterness seething in his mind. Cardowan had won, by a trick as cruel as it was cunning. He had outguessed and outsmarted Poco, and now he had the gold, all of it—and he left Poco only his life. But had he? Poco looked around him. This deep gorge, with its walls rising almost straight to the heavens, was a prison that would hold him until slow death by freezing had conquered.

And then everything in him revolted at the thought. As a last resort he could eat horsemeat to keep him alive. An extra gun and a rope were in his bedroll on the saddle. He'd always kept them there and they'd helped him out of many a tight spot before. The body of the horse would warm him for some hours yet.

He looked up the cliff. Up there somewhere was the trail, and the trail would lead him some day, somewhere to Espey Cardowan.

And meanwhile he must work.

CHAPTER SIX

Espey Cardowan walked over to the edge of the trail. He could see the scar in the snow where Poco's body struck first, but a jutting ledge cut off his vision. He could not see the bottom of the gorge, but he could see down far enough to make him draw back from the edge with an unpleasant feeling of dizziness. The cigarette was still in his mouth, and now he sucked it to life, inhaled, took it out of his mouth and examined it, chuckling.

"*Adios,* hard-case," he murmured. He hadn't expected such good fortune. Looking out over the mountains now, he was aware that relief can be one of the greatest physical pleasures known to man, and he felt it flood over him. He hadn't believed Poco's bluff about having men below, but still, what was there to prevent Poco from shoving him over a cliff and splitting the gold with his own gang waiting down there? Poco St. Vrain was slippery enough to, but he was gone now. And then it came to him that never again would he get that crawling feeling in his spine when those dark, unblinking eyes in that dourly arrogant face were turned on him. Never again would he watch those small hands and wonder if his were faster, knowing they weren't. Part of his relief lay in the fact that Poco St. Vrain lay in the bottom of the gorge, his back smashed, dying or dead. He would never walk again.

He flipped his cigarette away and examined the trail. Not a trace remained except for a loose rock, to show that a man and a horse had gone over the edge. He took the pack mule by the lead rope and started off down the trail, and now he was whistling.

All that afternoon as he threaded his precipitous way to safety, he kept thinking of the gold back there. It was his—or rather, it would soon be his. He had no idea of splitting it with that collection of saddle-bums down below that had sided him off and on for years. The first chance he got, he would sell them out to a bounty-hunting sheriff for his own freedom. Then wealth, land, cattle, women, wines, guns, horses, saddles—anything he wanted, and all of it he wanted. It would take a little cunning to swing it, but he had it.

When he swung into the last long stretch of trail before hitting the boulder fields below, it was getting late. He looked down over this gray and broken expanse and could see nothing, not a man. It puzzled and angered him at the same time. Had those damned fools got some whisky and drunk themselves into forsaking their guard? They had orders to post a tight guard where the trail ended.

He wondered about the lookout he had stationed a couple of yards up the trail. Would this man be drunk too?

And then he remembered Poco's brazen confidence, and he stopped short. Had Poco really had men down here all the time? In a frantic hurry Cardowan edged back to his horse and got his guns from the bedroll and strapped them on. He looked down again, and could see nothing. If Poco's men had driven his own off, then they would be guarding the trail end too.

He crouched now and made his way warily down the trail. Presently, in a twist of it ahead, he saw a man squatted behind a boulder. After a minute of careful scrutiny, he recognized Stony Pierson, his lieutenant. He approached openly now, and Stony, upon hearing him, turned and motioned him down. Almost on the heel of the gesture, Cardowan heard a rifle below him slash the silence, and a slug chipped some rock far overhead.

He crawled down to Stony, a squat, heavy man with a blue-black stubble of beard bulged out in one cheek by a wad of tobacco. He was squatted on his heels, a rifle across his knees, and there was a grim smile on his face as he watched Cardowan approach.

"What is it?" Cardowan asked when he was in the

shelter of the boulder.

Stony cuffed a greasy Stetson back off his forehead and spat. "Two-Way Hornbeck with a bunch. Been here since last night."

"Where are the boys?" Cardowan asked swiftly.

"Forted up behind rocks, same as Two-Way." This news given, Stoney asked, "Where's Poco?"

Cardowan did not answer him, only cursed.

"Where's Poco?" Stony asked again, unmoved.

"Dead. I got rid of him."

"Get the gold?"

"Up the trail around the bend."

Stony cursed now, too. "Well, boss," he said finally, "it looks like we split it. Two-Way's got a circle of men throwed around our bunch down there and we'll have to run them before we get away."

"Have you talked to him?"

Stony made a wry face. "He's talked to us. It's a two-way split, he says, or he'll stick until the men come down from the camp in behind us. We'll play hell gettin' away then."

Cardowan nodded, scowling.

"Leave it to Poco," Cardowan said bitterly. "That little pack of poison thought of everything."

"Not him," Stony answered. "This here was Two-Way's idea. He brung this bunch here to take it away from Poco. He said so hisself."

Cardowan cursed again in a kind of futile fury. Two-Way had him; there was no doubt about it. What worried him now was the extent of the split which Two-Way would demand. He knew Two-Way, knew him in person and by reputation. Mentally, he calculated his own share when the gold should be split in half, then divided again among the dozen men. It was scarcely more than he would get if he robbed the passengers in a stage.

He said, "We've got to parley with Two-Way."

Stony thought so too, but he added, "Let me go down. If Two-Way could hide behind a rock and cut down on you, he would."

Cardowan saw the truth in this. Between them they dug

up a soiled white handkerchief to use as a flag. "Get him
out in the open," Cardowan said, after Stony had waved
the flag tied on the end of his rifle barrel. "I'll go out, too,
at the same time. If anyone cuts down on me, you can get
him. And if you have to," he added bitterly, "gut shoot
him and leave him."

Stony smiled narrowly. "Yeah. We've had a taste of that
gut-shootin' already. Kirk is lying down there with a hole
in his belly now."

Cardowan nodded somberly. Stony rose in full view,
and he did not draw a fire. Cardowan watched as he
walked down the trail into the boulder field, and stopped
short. From behind a close boulder, another man rose and
came out to him, but the man was not Two-Way. After
a minute of parley Stony turned around, and Cardowan
guessed he was addressing their men, telling them to hold
their fire. Then Stony turned and waved to him.

Cardowan rose and walked down the trail. At the foot
of it he called to one of his men, visible now, and told him
the gold was up there and to watch it. Two-Way was
already standing erect a hundred yards away, and the two
men began to approach each other. Stony retreated now
behind a boulder.

Cardowan could see most of his men now, and he was
careful to walk forward out of earshot of the nearest. Two-
Way, dressed in his neat black and his white linen, took
his time in coming, and his half-smile was visible a long
way off. Cardowan leaned against a boulder.

When Two-Way was close, he took off his hat and
wiped the sweat from the sweatband.

"So it's you," he said easily. "Where's Poco?"

"I took care of him," Cardowan drawled.

Two-Way stared at him. "You're a liar," he said calmly.
"You couldn't."

"He's lying with a broken back up in one of those canyons. Do you see him with me?"

Two-Way shook his head, puzzled. "You mean you
killed him?"

"Pushed him over along with his horse."

"Did you see him dead?" Two-Way insisted.

"I couldn't see the bottom of the canyon, but I could see down two hundred feet. Figure it out for yourself."

Two-Way whistled low. "Was he drunk?"

"Listen," Cardowan said flatly, "Poco St. Vrain didn't have to be drunk to take a beating. He was scared. He crawled. He begged me, offered to throw in with me. He was yellow, and he got what a yellow coyote had coming."

Two-Way observed dryly, "He must be dead, then. You wouldn't talk that way if he was alive."

Cardowan's face turned a shade darker and he cursed Two-Way, who regarded him with patient attentiveness. When Cardowan was finished, Two-Way shrugged. "Well, that's a relief anyway. You did me a favor."

"Not on purpose."

"No," Two-Way said thoughtfully. "Now let's get down to business. Are those two mules packing the gold?"

Cardowan nodded.

"All right. I'll go away for one of them. Take your choice. It'll be a two-way split. If you don't agree, I'll roost here until Shayne and his men come down off the mountain. That won't be very funny, with men in front of you and men behind you."

Cardowan said it was agreeable to him, adding with a trace of admiration in his voice. "Nothing much gets past you, does it, Two-Way?"

"Not if I see it," Two-Way admitted.

"But something has already," Cardowan said, lowering his voice.

Two-Way said nothing, only looked at him.

Cardowan continued, "You mean you're going to take half this gold and be forced into a split-up with a bunch of saloon bums you picked up to corner me?"

Two-Way's eyes narrowed a little in his attempt to calculate the implications of Cardowan's hint.

"Are you?" Cardowan jibed.

"Now that you mention it," Two-Way said, "that's been troubling me for some time. The best I could do was to get three men out of my crew to help me in a getaway. But still it's a four-way split."

"Wouldn't you rather have the whole share?"

Two-Way smiled now. "Those are words, all right, but they don't make sense."

"Don't they?" Cardowan asked softly. "Throw in with me and they might."

Two-Way was already shaking his head. "I wouldn't trust you in the same county with me."

"And I wouldn't trust you in the same territory with me, if I could help it," Cardowan said. "We're both poison to each other. Every one of these men thinks that. Wouldn't it be a surprise if it turned out different?"

Two-Way was attentive now. He told him to go on.

Cardowan said, "I've got a man here I can trust. Stony Pierson. You get your best man. Let him in on this. It'll make four of us. Tonight we camp together and split up the gold. Tomorrow, you tell your men that you're trying to stick with me and my men on a chance that you may work us into a jackpot and take our share of the bricks. I'll tell my men the same. That'll leave us together for a couple of days until we work south."

"What's down there?"

Cardowan told him, smiling. Two-Way's face was immobile as he listened, and then he said softly, "Man, that'll take some gall."

"Is it worth a two-way split—more than you'd of got from Poco?" Cardowan asked shrewdly.

"I'd need clothes."

"Get them. I've got a man dying over here. You probably have too. Get theirs."

"I've got one dead," Two-Way said.

"Well?"

Two-Way laughed softly, his sardonic handsome face amused and lighted by some inner excitement. "Why not? Sure, I'll do it."

Cardowan said, "Remember. Act like you don't trust me even a little."

"Hell, I don't," Two-way replied.

Cardowan smiled meagerly, turned and called, "Come

out, men."

Two-Way did the same. When the twenty-four men were assembled, they made an unlovely crew. Cardowan's, on the whole, were a little less ragged, a little more intelligent appearing, since their profession provided well for them. Two-Way's oufit was a motley collection of riff-raff, with a scattering of boys and old men, the scum he had been able to recruit on the sly, who would fight or kill for a full belly and enough to get drunk on.

Two-Way spoke to them all. "Poco St. Vrain's dead and the gold is up on the trail. We'll camp down at timberline together and split up the gold. One of Espey's men and you, Pride, go up and get the mules. We'll wait for you."

Stony was sent along with Pride, a slim, surly man in his early twenties who had the nervous mannerisms, the pallor and the haunted eyes of a man who was happy only when half-full of liquor.

The cavalcade of mounted men reached timberline after dark, and a great roaring fire was built while two men were detailed to rustle up the grub. If Cardowan wanted to keep both sides at sword's points, he soon saw that it would not be difficult. His own men were sullen and angry while Two-Way's were suspicious to the point of silence. Immediately when camp was made they took opposite sides of the fire, and watched each other. Once the meal was over a tarp was spread on the ground by the fire, and the gold, which had remained in the two *aparejos* midway between them, was counted out. The sacks, weighed by a crude scale consisting of a straight split log balanced on a sharp rock, were weighed and adjusted to the satisfaction of the whole crowd.

That finished, each group withdrew a ways from the fire to gossip among themselves. Cardowan's wounded man, Kirk, was made comfortable and his wants attended to, although he was sunk in fever and was sure to die.

It was then that both Cardowan and Two-Way, their voices hushed, told their men, with occasional sidelong glances across the fire, of the plan. Why not stick with the other gang for a while and the opportunity might pre-

sent itself to get the rest of the gold? Two-Way's men
flushed with easy success, agreed. Cardowan's, still smart-
ing under the memory of the last two days, agreed too.

Guards were posted at the gold, around which the men
slept, and at the horses, and the camp settled for the
night.

Next morning at breakfast it was Two-Way who made
the proposition. What did Cardowan think of both
bunches traveling together? Word was bound to leak out
as to why they had come up here, and any bunch of wild
punchers could gang up to try and take the stuff away.
Why not stick together until they were out of the country?

Cardowan considered this, as if reluctant to give the
word. Then he drawled, eyeing his own men shrewdly,
"Maybe there's sense in that, boys. What do you say?"

They agreed, stifling their grins. Two-Way's men looked
at each other and smiled secretly. Two-Way and Cardowan also looked at each other, but neither smiled. They
were too good actors.

Before breaking camp the dead man was taken above
timberline and stones were piled over him. Two-Way took
the dead man's clothes and left his own. Kirk, who had
lived through the night, was sunk in a profound unconsciousness. His pulse was feeble, his breathing ragged.

Cardowan watched him for several minutes, then looked
up at the others.

"He can't live. And we can't take him. A mile of travel
would kill him."

He wanted to be generous now, and reasonable. Nothing should antagonize the men. Another time he would
have said curtly that they would leave him. Now he
wanted one of them to say it.

"Can't we leave grub and water and a hobbled horse
beside him?" one of the men asked.

Cardowan said they could, and that it was the only reasonable thing to do. "He's beyond help. He'll die."

It was settled that way. They left him in the shade,
food and water beside him, blankets over him, a note
pinned to them saying they had left a horse.

Two-Way watched this little play and approved it. He had a smart man in his new partner.

CHAPTER SEVEN

Poco set to work to make as much use as possible of the daylight left him. Digging out the bedroll he got his rope, then he beat his way through the snow to the trail side of the gorge. Thirty feet up on its side, a sharp point of rock stuck out through the snow—the rock he had barely scraped in passing. Since his rope was a thirty-foot one, it meant he would have to get part way up the gorgeside to rope the rock and it took him a good bit of the afternoon to make ten feet. Once that high, he cast his rope a hundred times before it settled finally over the point of rock. Testing it, he found the rock solid, and scaled the wall until he reached it.

Here he was checked. The only rock above within reach of his rope was thirty yards to his left, but from that rock he thought he could reach a narrow ledge several yards above it which he could see now. The time till dark he spent in scraping and packing hard a tortuous trail through the thick snow of the gorge face to a point almost below the rock. Just as it was getting dusk, the snow under his feet gave way and he tobogganed down into the gorge again.

He picked himself up and looked up at his work and smiled. A night of freezing would lock the hard-packed snow. Tomorrow morning he could use it.

He was exhausted and ravenous, but the thought of butchering his sorrel for food gagged him. He packed the snow hard between the outstretched legs of the horse, threw down his blankets, wrapped himself up in them, hugging the still-warm body of the horse, and was soon asleep.

He wakened before sunup, stiff and shivering, but the night of rest had restored some of his strength. By sunup, he had climbed the rope, freed it, coiled it, traveled the narrow trail, and was waiting, shivering, for full light to make his cast for the rock overhead. He accomplished this just after daylight, and pulled himself up to it. Here the cliff was almost perpendicular, and out of a thousand perilous casts with his rope, he looped a dozen pieces of ledge that stuck up through the snow—and every one of them pulled loose and thundered down into the gorge. But by noon he had looped a solid-looking one far to his right. It had taken every inch of his rope, and he knew that he had not tested it properly, but it was his only chance.

Looking below now, he wondered if the fall would kill him, and he decided it would not if he could dodge the avalanche. Taking a twist of the rope around his wrist, he swung off in a great ragged, pendulum swing—and the rock held.

It took the last bit of his strength to pull himself up to the ledge, and he lay on its warm bareness for ten long minutes, getting his breath and his strength back. Hand over face, he closed his eyes and let the sun warm him. It was then that he felt a light tap on his stomach. He opened his eyes and saw a small pebble lying on his shirt. For a minute, he just stared, and then he comprehended that this had fallen from above, way above.

Twisting to his knees, he whipped out a gun and fired into the air. He strained his eyes towards the vast sloping expanse of snow towering above him, and shot again.

And then, seemingly out of the snow itself, far above he saw a head emerge—the head of Kate Shayne.

For a moment he only stared, and then he waved. She was far above him—how far he could not guess—but he knew the first surge of hope.

"Your rope!" he called. He saw her nod and her head disappeared. Presently a rope began to trail down to him, and then it stopped, far, far, short. Before he could yell again the rope disappeared. Presently it came down again, long this time, but still almost fifty feet short. She doubtless had taken the pack rope off her pack horse.

He cast about him and saw that the ledge sloped up a little before it disappeared entirely. He worked his way to the very end, and it gave him almost five additional feet. Perhaps with his lariat he could make it.

He called up, "Take off your boot and put it in the loop."

The rope went up again. When it came down next, her boot, an object to rope, was in it. Too, it was longer, and Poco guessed she had cut the reins from her bridle, and tied them to the rope along with the saddle cinch. This time the boot was well within roping distance, and lying against the wall of snow, Poco set about to loop it. He did finally loop the toe of the boot, and it was on the fifty-seventh try in mid-afternoon.

He opened his mouth to call directions, but she seemed to understand. She pulled the rope up, his own hooked on the toe of her boot. Presently the whole thing was lowered again, and this time tied and minus the reins. He could just reach it. He waited until she anchored it and signaled him, and then he looked up. He was weak from hunger now, but a sort of desperation gave him strength. His jaw clamped shut and he began the ascent. The snow, due to the sharp angle of the slope was not so deep here, and the first half of the climb he negotiated easily. But he was tiring. He knew he was, but some deep bottom of his will made him go on although his arms were leaden, turned to syrup with fatigue. When he could go no farther, he twisted the rope in his foot and rested.

"Can you make it?" he heard Kate ask him from above. To save his breath he only nodded and shut his eyes to fight off the dizziness that was blinding him. When he had his strength back he looked up. It seemed miles until he would reach the trail, but he took the weight of his body off the rope, untwisted his leg, and started again. It was a fight, a dogged, strangling fight, and he did not look up, only guessed what was left as foot by foot he climbed.

Finally when he knew that he could go no farther he heard a voice say close above him, "If you can make it another two feet I'll get your wrists."

He did, but he never knew how. He only knew that after an eternity of struggling he felt two wire-taut hands grab him by the wrists.

"I'll try to hold one wrist while I make a loop," she said.

He nodded.

The rope was pulled up under him for a way, there was a pause, and she said, "Push away and let it slide down under you."

He did.

"The loop is just below your knee," she said.

He felt for it and got it with his foot and the weight slacked off. In another moment, after he had rested, he climbed the rest of the way with her aid.

Once up he sat on the trail, his head hung on his chest, his sight swimming. He was aware that she was half-dragging him until his back rested against the wall. Presently he felt a biscuit thrust into his hand and he ate it in two swallows, and took the canteen she gave him and gulped three deep swallows before it was yanked away.

"You'll get more later," she said, and he sensed now how emotionless and flat her voice was.

"Can you talk?" she asked after a while.

He looked up at her, and he could see her frown. He knew his face was cut, caked with blood and sweat, and that his clothes were in rags and his hands a bloody pulp.

He said huskily. "Yes, enough to thank you."

"What happened?" she asked.

Poco's glance evaded hers. He said nothing, and she said sharply, "What happened. Did you fall off?"

Poco heaved a deep sigh. Slowly he drew out his gun and laid it on his lap, and said, "I was shoved over with my horse."

He knew it had to be faced sometime, that she had to know, and some dim instinct of self-preservation told him that while he didn't mind the inevitable punishment, he would not accept it before he killed Cardowan.

Kate said, "By Shelton?"

"He's not Shelton," Poco said quietly. "He's Espey Cardowan. I'm not Jacob Finger, either."

"I know," she said quietly. "You're Poco St. Vrain, aren't you?"

He looked up at her curiously. "How did you know?"

"I guessed it," she said dully.

"Then why did you help me up?"

"I would have done the same for a dog," she said, her voice flat and toneless and weary.

Poco watched her, saw the look of loathing in her face, and for once he was humble. He wanted to crawl off, to hide, to get away from the silent accusation in her eyes.

She said, looking out over the ragged mountains of rock that tumbled away on all sides of them, "The gold is gone, of course—stolen."

"Yes." He did not look at her until he heard her sobbing quietly, and he saw that her back was to him, and that she was fingering the mane of her horse, who was standing quietly and alertly watching this.

Poco cleared his throat. "What's it to you?" he asked curiously. "The gold belongs to Abe McCandless."

She said bitterly, "You know him. Do you think they'll pay Dad a cent for this year's work when they find out how he was fooled?"

"You've been fed and clothed. There are other jobs."

She whirled on him, her face cold with fury. "You blind fool! Do you think Abe McCandless will let it go at that! Didn't Dad advise sending for an insurance company to take out the gold? Didn't he tell McCandless not to interview the agents? Didn't he ask for secrecy, for a lone hand in all this? Do you think McCandless will believe you had the right credentials and that Dad wasn't hand in glove with you? Do you think he won't go to prison—or that you haven't ruined his life and made it impossible for him to get other work?"

Poco considered this a moment in silence, staring at the gun in his lap. He had gone into this a lone wolf, like he went into everything, to work his own will and be damned to the world. And now, for the first time in his life, he saw how it worked out for other people.

It puzzled him. He figured it was evening part of the score with Abe McCandless, and here were two innocent people, Kate Shayne and her father, who would suffer the most. McCandless wouldn't be harmed; he had money enough as it was.

And then he wondered with his old arrogance why he should care. What did he owe the Shaynes, the weak fools? And then he paused. What did he owe them? Only his life.

A dark and uncomfortable shame crept over him at the thought. And then everything that it implied came unbidden into his mind. The Shaynes would bear the blame for this, while he, the thief, rode off. He denied it to himself, but there it was, and he had to face it.

He sifted a handful of gravel through his fingers, then looked up at Kate.

"I can get that gold back," he said quietly.

Her lip curled, and the contempt in her face was keen and cold and without pity.

"You wouldn't if you could—and you can't."

Poco felt anger well up in him. He tried to get to his feet, and it took him a long time, while she did not help, only watched him.

"Listen," he said. "I said I can get that gold back."

"You can't even steal it for yourself."

Poco flushed.

"A poor, weak thief doesn't turn into a decent strong man overnight!" Kate said coldly. "You're arrogant because you have to be, because you have to assure yourself you're as good as other thieves—as good as Cardowan."

Poco said in a thick voice, "There's not a man living would say that to me."

"Because you would either run or shoot him," Kate said. "You've got gun-courage. It's like whisky-courage. Any man can have it. You've got a gun in your hand now, you drew it when you had to face a showdown with a woman."

Poco said narrowly, "That was because I won't be caught—not by you, not by any woman, not by any man, until I settle this score with Cardowan."

"And get the gold and spend it, while my father rots in jail for your crime."

"I said I would get it back for you—not for McCandless! For you!"

"You lie!" Kate said coldly.

Poco holstered his gun, his face white with anger.

"Maybe I lie, then," he said. "If I do or if I don't, you're not going back to the camp."

"I don't intend to," she said. "I'll ride to Abe McCandless with news of this. I can spare my father that, anyway."

"I'll search your outfit first," Poco said tonelessly. She stood aside while he searched the bedroll and the contents of the pack on the second horse. He found a six-gun in the bedroll, and he plugged out all the shells then put it back. He worked slowly, beaten with fatigue, but his face was arrogant. When the horse was packed, he said, "Lead off."

Kate did not move. She had been watching him all this while with an aloof contempt she took no pains to hide. She said now, "Let's get this straight. Do you think I have any claim on your life?"

"Yes."

She nodded. "Don't be surprised if I try and take it."

CHAPTER EIGHT

CARDOWAN GOT A CHANCE to talk alone with Stony that afternoon. Stony was Cardowan's man anyway, body and soul, and Cardowan had an easy time getting his consent to betrayal compared with the argument Two-Way had with Pride. But Two-Way was a better talker, and by use of a little judicious blackmail, Pride was willing to betray not only all of Two-Way's bunch, but the other two whom Two-Way had already bribed.

They clung to the timber all day, traveling south high in the San Jons. In midafternoon, however, Two-Way and Cardowan, by mutual and open agreement, decided to head down for the foothills and split up the next day.

They camped that night in the timber of the foothills. When camp was made Cardowan ordered the gold pack removed from the mule so that he could be fed and watered. Then, he directed, the pack was to be placed again on the mule. To his inquisitive men he explained in a low voice, "I don't trust that crew. This is the last night. Why take a chance? If we sleep with the gold beside us, what's to stop them from pretending they're asleep, then cutting down on us while we are ? If the gold is kept together on the pack mule and put behind us and guarded by Stony, here, they'll have to wake us before they can get to it. If they sleep with their gold beside them we can pretend we are sleeping and get it. We'll wait and see."

They agreed. Strangely enough, Two-Way privately made the same proposition to his men. Dressed in the ragged, soiled clothes of the dead man, Two-Way still had his old suavity and persuasiveness, and his men agreed to the same. His proposition about raiding the other bunch in their sleep was identical to Cardowan's, so that when both outfits kept their pack mule loaded, it was a stalemate. They cursed each other under their breaths, but rolled in and were soon asleep.

Cardowan put a guard over the camp as an added precaution, but Two-Way did not.

Both Cardowan and Two-Way slept far back from the fire, the closest to the horses. Close to midnight, when the whole camp was sleeping, except for Pride, Stony and the guard, Cardowan suddenly sat up. Coker, the guard, squatting by the fire, saw him immediately, and Cardowan put a finger to his lips and beckoned. Coker came to his side, and Cardowan rose, putting on his boots. As soon as they had backed away from the sleeping men, Cardowan said, "Did you hear anything funny?"

Coker said no.

"Let's take a *pasear* out by those horses."

"Hell, you're gettin' spooked, boss. Stony's out there."

"I know. Still it won't hurt to look."

Cardowan led off into the darkness. Their horses were thrown together in a rope corral back in a cleared spot in the timber. Halfway to them Cardowan said, "I still hear it. Like a man thrashing on the ground."

Coker came close and listened.

"Stand over here," Cardowan said.

Coker stepped over. Slowly Cardowan raised the six-gun in his hand, poised it a moment over his head, then brought it down in a swooping full arc that ended on Coker's head. Coker went limp and melted to the ground.

He paused long enough to wipe the gun barrel on Coker's shirt, then he made his way to the corral.

Stony loomed out of the night.

"Got the pack on the horse?"

"Sure. Your horse and mine are saddled."

"Where?"

Stony disappeared, and led them all out.

Cardowan said, "We'll wait a minute."

"What for?"

"Give Two-Way time."

"Where's Coker?"

Cardowan said disgustedly, "Hell, he was sleeping by the fire."

They waited without talking, and then splintering the silence of the night with its roar, came the stuttering fire of a gun. Three shots.

Stony said, "Goddlemighty, what's that?"

Cardowan, in that second of thunder, had drawn his gun, and now he said, "It's this, Stony."

His gun was three inches from Stony's chest, and he let it off twice. Stony clawed out at him, but the second shot drove him back and down. Cardowan held his gun, ripped loose the rope corral, mounted, held the lead rope of the pack horse, then emptied his gun into the horses in the corral. There was a wild milling and snorting and screaming of stampeding animals, and Cardowan moved away from them through the timber. In a moment, the horses would be scattered he knew. He smiled faintly at the thought that he had betrayed a betrayer.

Traveling slowly east for three minutes or so, long after the last sounds of the uproar in camp had faded, he picked his way through the trees. Presently, bearing left, he approached the bank of a wash. He traveled this for another minute, whistling a low clear note every few seconds.

When he got an answer he spurred on ahead.

Two-Way was waiting, his pack animal bulking large

in the dark.

From behind a tree came Two-Way's voice. "Throw both guns away, Espey."

Cardowan said, "Where are you?"

"Wouldn't you like to know? I said, throw them away. It was part of the bargain."

"All right. Listen."

Two-Way listened, and he heard the crash of a gun thrown in brush.

"Now yours," Cardowan said.

Two-Way threw away his gun and Cardowan heard the crash. The procedure was repeated again, and only then did Two-Way walk out of the darkness.

"Now we've got to ride."

"Did you get your horses stampeded?" Cardowan asked.

"Hell, yes. They broke loose when I shot Pride."

"That'll give us a couple of hours anyway."

"And we'll need it."

They rode side by side, leading their pack horses. Soon, under thin moonlight, they hit rolling grasslands.

"Straight on," Cardowan said. "We can't miss it."

Another hour of riding and they came across a wagon road, which they took, still headed south.

"How far?" Two-Way asked.

"We'll make it by daylight if we aren't crowded."

The going was slow, in spite of the fact that the weary pack mules had been exchanged by Stony and Pride for the strongest horses, for the packs weighed two hundred and fifty pounds each. Cardowan whistled softly to cover up his impatience, while Two-Way rode silently. If either of them was recalling that he had betrayed his men with the aid of another man, whom he had betrayed in turn, he said nothing.

Two-Way spoke only once during the ride, and then he said, "You better shed those holsters and belts. Remember, we're prospectors without guns."

Cardowan complied. As the time drew out, Two-Way became restless. Occasionally he would stop and Cardowan would pull up ahead while Two-Way listened.

"Is there a man in your bunch that's got brains enough to think of this?"

"Not with Stony dead."

Two-Way grunted and spurred on.

When they finally topped a low ridge and saw lying below them in the moonlight a small cluster of buildings, Two-Way pulled up again.

"Two miles more," Cardowan said.

Two-Way said, "Quiet."

They both listened. Riding on a gentle wind at their backs they could hear the far tattoo of horses at a gallop.

"Hear it?"

"Come on," Cardowan said, and roweled his horse. It soon became apparent that they would have to drive the two pack horses ahead, and as soon as they were through the half-dozen buildings of the tiny settlement below, they dropped behind.

The road lay straight ahead, so that the going was easy, but still they dragged.

"They'll be tired," Cardowan called.

"And not a gun between us," Two-Way yelled savagely.

Drawing out on the plain now they could look behind and see a cluster of spots that were men pursuing them, and they cursed impotently.

When the sound of the first shot rode down to them on the wind, they leaned over in their saddles and spurred up beside the two pack horses. Two-Way lashed out with his rope in a frantic endeavor to put the speed of fear in the laden horses, but they were running their best.

After an eternity, in which the shots behind increased in volume and number, they saw a squat, flat rectangle on the moonlit prairie ahead.

"We'll make it," Two-Way exulted.

And in another minute they were approaching the gates of Fort Benjamin.

The two pack horses, blown and almost foundered, thundered into the high arch of the gateway and pulled up in a moil of dust before the closed gates. From a grill in the thick gate a sentry's voice challenged them.

"Who is it?" he ripped out.

Two-Way said rapidly, "Open up, for God's sake, friend, and let us inside; We're a couple of prospectors being chased by Poco St. Vrain and his gang!"

As if to punctuate his plea, a slug ripped into the dobie wall high above the sentry's head.

"But it's against—"

"To hell with your orders!" Two-Way cut in harshly. "Do you want two innocent men shot down because the commandant isn't awake?"

The gates swung open enough to admit the horses, which Two-Way and Cardowan hazed through under a growing hail of fire. Inside, a running man passed them, and with the help of the sentry closed the massive gates and barred them. Already there was a scattering of men climbing the ladders that led to the top of the high, five-foot thick adobe walls, and lights appeared on two sides of the square where the barracks lay.

Two-Way and Cardowan pulled up and dismounted inside. There was a racket of gunfire outside, and the reply of the soldiers was swelling as more armed men swarmed to their posts.

Cardowan said, "Rub dirt on your hands and face. I'll get the horses." He paused. "Think you can swing it?"

"I'll have him crying on my shoulder," Two-Way said.

A belated bugle call rang through the fort. Two-Way now had a chance to observe the place. The fort was a long rectangle, rooms against the outer wall facing the center and shadowed by a porch that ran along all four sides. At the rear the walls were higher, and in one corner a big two-story building merged into the moon shadow.

Cardowan returned with the pack horses, just as the sentry came.

"Leave those horses and come with me," he ordered.

"Leave them hell!" Two-Way snorted. "Those horses are loaded with gold."

The soldier a long gangly lad, said quietly, "We're soldiers here, mister."

"Don't soldiers use money?" Two-Way asked.

"Not if they have to steal it," the soldier replied. "Come along."

They followed his blue-clad figure across the hard-packed square to a room next the two-story building. A light burned in the room, and the sentry was challenged by a guard at the door. Before he could answer, a voice called out from the room: "Come in, Hardy."

Two-Way and Cardowan preceded the sentry into a bare, neat room, containing a desk, a cabinet, a half-dozen chairs and several military pictures on the white-washed wall. Flags were furled in the corner.

Behind the desk in shirt sleeves, his hair rumpled, his eyes squinting against the sudden lamplight, stood a tall bearded man with kindly, curious eyes.

He said, "Gentlemen," looking from Two-Way and Cardowan back to Two-Way. Then he looked at the sentry, who had saluted. He raised a careless finger in acknowledgment and said, "Well, Hardy?"

"These two men rode up at a gallop, sir. There were others behind them shooting. They claimed Poco St. Vrain and his gang were chasing them, and they asked for shelter. I shut the gates, sir."

"Poco St. Vrain, you say?" the major asked slowly.

Two-Way said humbly. "Yes, sir."

The major said to the trooper, "Tell Lieutenant Cooper to report immediately."

Hardy no more than saluted and stepped out of the door when a brisk young man, his blue coat buttoned awry, appeared and saluted.

"That's St. Vrain," the major said simply. "Take a detail of twenty men and chase him until you get him."

When the lieutenant had disappeared, the major said to Two-Way, "What was he chasing you for?"

"We're a couple of prospectors turned miners, sir. We operated a small mine and mill up in the mountains through the winter. Last week we paid off our crew, closed the mine and set out with our winter's stake. We'd struck it pretty rich and St. Vrain must have heard about it. We were traveling at night with our gold. Tonight as we passed through this town—those houses—"

"Where the concessionaires live?"

"Yes, I guess so. When we passed through there he set out after us. We knew about the fort, and reckoned you'd give us some help."

The major contemplated the two before him. Two-Way was unshaven, his mustache ragged, his hands black, his clothes little better than tatters. Cardowan was a cool, lanky, unwashed and unshaven man, who kept a respectful silence. They seemed to need help, and that was what the army was for in this country. The major's face relaxed.

"Glad to help. Did they get your gold?"

"No, sir, it's outside on our pack horses."

"Pack horses?" the major echoed, emphasizing the plural. "You must have a lot."

"About five hundred pounds," Two-Way said calmly.

"Of gold?"

"Yes, bullion."

The major smiled now. "Well, congratulations on your good luck. You're rich men."

A man came in at this moment and reported. St. Vrain's men, sensing what was in store, had ceased fire, banded together and ridden off. Lieutenant Cooper had just left with the detail. The major nodded and dismissed him.

"Well, I reckon we better ride on," Two-Way said in an excellent imitation of the homely speech of a mountain man. "He's high-tailed it now."

"Ride where?" the major said.

Two-Way grinned pleasantly. "I dunno. Anywhere where we can get to a Wells Fargo stage."

"Not tonight?"

"We wouldn't be no trouble, Major," Two-Way said diffidently. "You've given us a lift and we're obliged."

"Nonsense," the major said gruffly. "We'll put you up here tonight and send a guard along with you tomorrow. Why, good Lord, man, you can't ride the country with a fortune rolling around loose in your packs. You'd be robbed before you got a mile from here."

Two-Way looked at Cardowan, "Reckon that's right,

Curt."

"Reckon it is," Cardowan drawled.

"We wouldn't want to be no trouble," Two-Way said humbly.

The major laughed in spite of himself, and called to the guard outside. "Take these men over to the barracks and see they get beds and whatever else they need. And bring the packs from those two horses in here."

The major bid them good night, refused their thanks, and dismissed them.

Once in the barracks, which were not unlike a bunkhouse, a series of connected rooms with bunks from ceiling to floor, Two-Way and Cardowan thanked their guard, bid him good night and started to undress. The room had been emptied of soldiers, who had ridden out with Lieutenant Cooper, so they had it to themselves.

Two-Way looked at Cardowan and smiled faintly.

Cardowan shook his head in open admiration. "Two-Way, you and me could get somewhere together."

Two-Way laughed silently. "Did you ever see a coyote team up with a wolf? They're both dogs, but they don't run together."

Cardowan said, "Which one's the wolf?"

Two-Way said, "You can make a noise like one. I can think like one. You can fight like one. I can run like one. The only wolf I ever knew is dead now, and God help us if his ghost walks. We'll both be coyotes then." He tumbled into a bunk. 'The army's a wonderful institution," he said thoughtfully, chuckling softly. "I'll remember this when I need help again."

CHAPTER NINE

I T WAS DARK before Kate and Poco hit the boulder fields, but since it was impossible to camp here in this windswept desert, they went on. Now that they could ride again, Kate halted and shifted the pack from her pack horse to her saddle horse, so that Poco might have a mount.

He accepted reluctantly, thanking her briefly. It would have been impossible for him to reach timberline afoot, for he was so exhausted he was gray around the mouth. He mounted and led off.

Just at timberline he swung off the trail to a creek he remembered, and surprised a horse that was watering there. The horse was hobbled, and it shied away at the approach of their horses. Poco went after it, and got it.

Kate was waiting when he returned, and she said, "Whose is it?"

"Likely one from Cardowan's bunch," he replied, but he wondered. The horse was a chunky bay, valuable even to a man who would share in a fabulous amount of gold.

They followed the creek down until they came to a sort of flat clearing where they dismounted. The place was shadowed, and Poco looked around it, then jumped the stream heading for a big pine whose lower twigs would furnish dry tinder to start the fire.

He had broken several off when he heard a faint voice close to him say, "Who is it?"

Poco whirled, his hand dropping to his gun. He waited a long time, then said, "Where are you?"

Kate heard the voice and she crossed the creek too, now. Poco said to her, "Stay where you are."

He went down towards the stream, laid the twigs down, and put a match to them. By their growing light he could see a blanketed figure under a tree away from the stream. Laying some more wood on the fire, he and Kate walked over to it. A canteen, some jerky and guns lay beside the man next to a saddle. Poco knelt by him.

"What happened, fella?" Poco asked gently. Then he saw the note left on the blanket and he read it. It said there was a hobbled horse near.

The man studied Poco's face in frowning concentration. "You're St. Vrain," he whispered.

Poco nodded. "You belong with Cardowan's outfit?"

When the man nodded too, Kate said softly, "Did he shoot you?"

The man shook his head slowly. "Two-Way Hornbeck's

bunch. They surprised us. We fought and I got it."

"Where?"

The man pointed to his stomach. "I'd like a drink," he whispered wearily.

Poco said, "No good, fella. It'll hurt worse than being thirsty."

The man smiled faintly. "Hell, I'll die anyway. I don't want to die thirsty."

Poco looked up at Kate and she looked away.

"All right," he said.

"I'll get it," Kate told him. She took the canteen down to the creek, while Poco learned what had happened. He listened to the broken recital of the wounded man, and from it pieced together the fact that Two-Way and Cardowan had made a truce, and that they split the gold and left.

When Kate came back with the canteen, Poco said to the man, "This'll hurt. And it won't help your thirst."

"Give it to me."

Poco put it to his mouth and let him sip it. After the first deep swig, the man turned his head away, and Poco saw his face screw up in agony. He watched a little longer, and then he saw that the man was unconscious. He said to Kate, "He'll die. He's been like this since last night."

"Isn't there anything we can do?" she asked.

Poco shook his head. "When they get it there, they're done. I hope the water kills him."

When she looked up at him, surprise in her face, he said, "You'd spare a horse that, wouldn't you?"

She nodded faintly and turned away. Poco staked out all three horses while she prepared the meal. It was a scant one, not meant for two, and Poco ate sparingly and in silence, his face brooding and impassive. Kate too was somber and silent, and Poco, remembering what she had said that afternoon, avoided looking at her. When they were finished eating Poco went over to look at the wounded man. He was still unconscious, breathing faintly. Poco took his guns, plugged out the shells, put them in his shell belt, then came back to the fire.

Kate had been watching him, and she said, "Why did

you do that?"

"Something you said up there on the trail."

"About you owing me your life?"

"Yes. But I don't owe it yet. I've got to settle some things."

"What?"

Poco said without looking at her, "Get the gold. Get even with Cardowan—and with Two-Way."

"Who is Two-Way?"

Poco said, letting no life into his voice, "The man that got me the papers from the agent. The man that killed the agent. The man I was to split with."

"Did you come this far with him?"

"No. He doublecrossed me. He was waiting here to take the gold away from me when I came down."

Kate looked at him wonderingly. "And yet you run with these men, trust them. Why are you such a fool?"

Poco said, "Why not? They're open. They don't claim to be anything else. You know where you stand with them, because you know they'll doublecross you, kill you, do anything to you if there's a piece of money in it for them. They don't hide behind a handshake and a smile."

"Did you guess Two-Way would try to take the gold from you?"

"Not right away. I figured he couldn't get the men together to do it."

"Men?" Kate echoed. "Couldn't he do it alone?"

Poco said, "Three like him couldn't," and there was no boasting in his tone.

" 'And the meek shall inherit the earth,' " Kate quoted.

"How much of it do they own now?" Poco countered.

"Enough to be content."

Poco said slowly, staring at the fire, "That's what I thought once, too. But I soon learned different. You'd like to see me meek. All right, I get meek. I ride into a town— any town—the county seat. I go in a saloon for a drink. In two minutes, the sheriff walks in. He doesn't draw a gun, see, because I'm not meek and he knows it, but if I was, he'd draw one. He'd take me over to his office. He'd put me in a chair and stick a gun in my face and he'd say, 'I want a confession that you robbed the Sacaton National Bank last week. Sign this paper.' I'm meek. I was seven counties to the west when that bank was robbed and I tell him so. He cocks his gun and says, 'Sign it.' If I won't he lets the gun off in my face and collects about three thousand dollars bounty. If I do sign it, I get a fake trial and ten years in the pen."

"And if you aren't meek?" Kate said.

"I walk into the saloon and the sheriff doesn't draw a gun on me. He asks me to go with him. I do. I don't sit down, I stand there and let him sweat trying to figure out how to ask me questions he knows will make me mad. He asks me questions. I lie, and he knows I lie, but he doesn't say so. He gets sort of a cold feeling in his stomach after a while and he says that's all. He buys me a drink and lets me ride out of town, hoping I'll clear his county before trouble happens. See the difference?"

"Yes, but there must have been a beginning to this. If you were guiltless in the first place he'd never ask you in. How did it start? You must have been to blame."

Poco looked at her with hot eyes, his lip curling up in a sneer. "If I don't come back with the gold and your dad goes to jail for it, ask him that. You won't miss it far."

He got up and walked off into the night. When he came back Kate was rolled up in her blankets. One of them was set aside for him to use. He laid it over her, then went over to the wounded man, and saw that he was sunk deep in unconsciousness.

Rolling up in the tarp Poco was immediately asleep. He woke an hour before dawn and got up and rinsed his face in the cold water of the stream, then built up the fire. Kate was sleeping soundly. He went over to the wounded man and saw immediately that he was dead.

Picking him up Poco carried him up above timberline and piled rocks on him. When he returned, Kate was still sleeping. Poco took the dead man's blankets and saddle, and leaving a handful of shells for Kate, stepped out of the circle of firelight to the horses. Dawn was breaking as he saddled the dead man's horse. He was ready to mount, even had his foot in the stirrup when he paused, and withdrew it. Walking back to the camp, he crossed the cleared space and stood by Kate, who was still sleeping.

He looked at her a long time, wondering many things. This was a girl who had no cause to treat him kindly, who had even cause to hate and loathe him, even kill him. Yet she had treated him kindly, shared her food and her blankets with him, and still, underneath it all, was a hardness, a bedrock distaste for his soiled way of life. She would do everything in her power to bring him to justice, but she would go about it like a person who knows only a stern set of rules and what they demand. No whimpering, no cursing, no cunning or trickery, just a serene adherence to a code that he sneered at and did not recognize.

Some people when they sleep seem to die, to relax utterly and finally, to deflate the spirit, so that they are a shell, waiting for the life wakefulness brings, but looking at her now, Poco saw she was not like this. Her face was serene, not slack, and it held life in it, as if she were only lying there with closed eyes.

He tried to remember the last words she had spoken to him, and he could. "You must have been to blame." Turning away, he wondered if he was, and then he knew he wasn't, and he smiled sardonically at himself as he walked over to his horse.

It was light enough now so that he could pick up the tracks of the cavalcade that preceded him. He clung to the same route high in the San Jons, and he traveled fast.

Noon found him at the second camp of Two-Way and Cardowan, and two fresh graves pointed to something he could not immediately understand. But investigation showed him that there had been turmoil here, and that everyone did not leave at the same time. But, strangely enough, they all took the same route, which led out due east until it hit the road, then turned south.

By midafternoon he was atop the rise that looked down on the buildings of the concessionaires, who were not allowed to raise their establishments on military ground.

He knew the place, knew Joe Hannigan that ran the saloon. He could see some blue-coated troopers, and remembering his tangle with the commandant at Fort Benjamin, decided not to show himself too openly.

He stayed behind the ridge till it flattened out in a clump of screening cottonwoods. This grove touched the cluster of buildings in back of Hannigan's frame saloon. He dismounted and walked through the back lot.

Joe Hannigan had two rooms built on the rear and one side of his saloon, and it was for there Poco headed. The door was unlocked. Stepping inside he almost bumped into a Mexican woman who was cleaning up the bedroom. She looked at him suspiciously.

"Get Joe," he said.

The woman was used to this kind of visit, and she uttered, *"Sí"* sullenly, and went out through the door that led to the small kitchen and the rear of the saloon.

In a moment a man stepped through the door to the bedroom. He was in shirt sleeves, fat, bald-headed, with wary small eyes. He was wiping his hands on a soiled apron, but when he looked around the room and his glance fell on Poco, the movement of his hands died. Then he turned around and locked the door.

Poco said dryly, "It's no stick-up. Why the locked door?"

Joe replied in a deep voice, and just as dryly, "What's the matter, did they lock you out of the fort?"

Poco scowled. "I don't get it."

"You don't know a bunch of troopers are combing the hills for you?"

"Still?" Poco said. "They've got a long memory."

"You expect to bring a bunch of hard-cases up and try to take the fort in the middle of the night and have them forget it by morning?"

Poco said, "Slow down and say that again."

Joe repeated himself, adding, "You oughta had more sense than that, Poco. Why did you have to chase those two jaspers that way?"

"What two jaspers?"

"Them prospectors with their gold. You might of

known you'd lose it for good if they reached there. Why the hell did you have to shoot up the place?"

Suddenly Poco understood. Two-Way and Cardowan had stolen the gold from their own men, run for the fort, and then had thrown the blame on Poco, so that the troopers would drive the two gangs back into the hills. He had his mouth open to explain, but he saw it was unnecessary. Instead he said, "Where are they now, these prospectors?"

Joe shook his head. "I oughtn't to tell you. You never used to do things like that, Poco. Leave 'em be."

"You will tell me, though," Poco said quietly.

Joe nodded in resigned agreement. "Yeah. For five years I been tellin' you things that could get me hung higher'n a kite."

"Where are they?"

Joe shrugged. "The captain sent a guard along with them to Rincon this morning."

"A guard?" Poco repeated slowly. If it had been anyone else but Two-Way who had done this, Poco would not have believed it, but this had the unmistakable mark of Two-Way's brainwork—or Cardowan's. This hadn't been ordinary stealing. Five hundred pounds of gold cannot be snatched out of thin air and disappear the same way. And realizing this, Two-Way had first contrived to have the army chase off his own men, then give him safe-conduct out of the country. Poco smiled narrowly at the thought. He said, "I'd like to see that."

"See what?"

Poco lounged erect. "Some day, Joe," he said, smiling a little, "the army will buy you drinks to keep you from telling what suckers they are."

He left Hannigan standing scowling, wondering too.

CHAPTER TEN

A FTER A NIGHT and a half day in the saddle, hours which had taken him over the San Jons, skirting the pass, using every shortcut he knew in high country, Poco dismounted

by the trough at the livery stable in Rincon and doused
his face. Upstreet the town stretched out broiling in the
afternoon sun, smelling of dust and sun-scorched boards.

The boy who had taken Poco's horse and stalled him
was just across the center way and Poco strolled over.

"I'm looking to meet a couple of gents here. They were
packing two horses. Seen anything of 'em?"

The lad said he hadn't, and Poco sauntered out into
the street. He tried to recall if he had done anything in
this county that he would be wanted for, and he could
not. Besides, this was no time to count risks. He was about
to turn upstreet, when he stopped, his face thoughtful.
Returning to the stable he unbuckled one of his shell
belts with its pendant holster and gun. He slipped the
gun into the top of his boot, went over and hung the
shell belt on his saddle horn, then went outside and up
the street. This was his way of not crowding his luck, a
kind of offering to whatever gods looked after him.

The Maricopa Saloon lay across the way, a big two-
story affair that dominated the other buildings along
the dusty street. Poco, scanning the single avenue, noted
and remembered that the small shack on the cross street
ahead was probably the sheriff's office, because a long
dobie building with barred windows abutted it.

He swung under the tie rail, then paused to let a half-
dozen horsemen ride by him. Poco observed them carelessly, until his attention was yanked up by the figure of
Abe McCandless who was just now swinging into the tie
rail in front of the Maricopa.

For one brief moment he contemplated with a kind of
sardonic relish what would happen when Two-Way and
Cardowan drifted into this. He knew now that Kate
Shayne had not reached McCandless, and that McCandless would have no idea of what had happened upon the
mountain. In his incessant traveling from ranch to ranch,
from one vast holding to another, McCandless would ride
the legs off a horse in a week. And because he was always
moving, and because Poco was lucky and Kate Shayne
generous, this whole thing could come to a head here to-

night—only it wouldn't. The gold was to be returned to Kate, not McCandless.

Poco waited until McCandless was dismounted and on the walk, and then he called sharply, "Mac!"

Big Abe turned ponderously, as did most of his men. Poco started across the street, saying clearly, "Don't go in there. I'm going in. I don't want to look at you."

McCandless backed away from the door. Over his rugged and craggy face came that look of stern control which Poco had seen so often and which so delighted him. As Poco swung under the tie rail Mac backed into his men, who were lined up across the sidewalk.

"Is this it?" Mac asked quietly again.

Poco stopped and confronted them. "Not yet, Mac," Poco said gently. "I won't kill you now."

Mac nodded, much as he might have received any news of his business. Only his eyes betrayed his fear.

Poco laughed softly. "You've caught me with only one gun, Mac. You and your gunnies make your play, why don't you?"

McCandless only shook his head. Suddenly, one of his men cursed. "Is that the bogus badman, Mac? Let's get it over with." He was big, red-faced, sneering.

The man standing next to the speaker grabbed his arm and pulled him away. Another of McCandless's hands grabbed the red-faced man's other arm.

"Forget it, Poco," he said. "Hank's new."

"Sure," Poco said gently, arrogantly. "I could tell that."

He looked coolly at the lot of them, then shouldered through the batwing doors.

McCandless watched the door long after he had entered. One of the men who had grabbed his companion said bitterly, "You might of got us all killed."

The men shifted uneasily, waiting for word from McCandless. Slowly McCandless turned, his face utterly grim.

"Wait for me at the other saloon," he said curtly, and brushed through his men, going up the street.

At the sheriff's office on the corner he swung in, shutting the door behind him. A gaunt, cadaverous man who had been playing rummy with a younger, shorter, squatter man, leaped to his feet. They both did. The younger man wore the deputy's badge.

"Sit down!" McCandless ordered. He pulled a chair up to the table for himself and brushed the cards off it. Both men sank slowly to their seats.

"I've had enough of this," McCandless began thickly, tapping the table. "We'll have a showdown. Now. For once and all."

"Who with?" the sheriff asked uneasily. Over his face came that impassive, wary look of a man who expects to hear what he would rather not.

"St. Vrain. He's in town."

The sheriff exchanged a fleeting look with his deputy. "I've got a family," he said to Mac and cleared his throat so that his voice would not seem so ineffective.

"You've got a job, too," Mac said, his hot eyes on him. "Do you want to keep it?"

"Not that bad."

Mac's fingers ceased drumming on the table, and he said precisely, pitilessly, "Hogan, I put a star on you because you were my man, because you've got a back trail that stinks to high heaven. I'm not asking you, I'm telling you. You'll help me take St. Vrain or you'll spend the rest of your life on the dodge. And you better make it Canada because Mexico won't be far enough. Understand that?"

Sheriff Hogan swallowed. "Sure," he said, and when he realized that he had whispered the word, he cleared his throat again.

The deputy rose now and laid his badge on the table. "So long, Frank. It was a good job." He walked toward the door, and Mac did not even look at him as he went out.

"How many men can you raise here?" Mac asked Hogan. "None."

Mac laid both hands on the table, palms down. "Yes, you can," he said. "If I decided to freight my own stuff in here from the railroad this town would dry up. Tell those counter-jumpers that. I want fifteen of them and in damned short order. Let them bring their own guns."

"It won't work, Mac," Hogan said hoarsely. "I tell you I know. You ought to know. He'll get away, because the jail hasn't been built yet that will hold him. And if he gets away, he'll come back!"

"Kill him."

Hogan flared up. "Now that would be bright. I wouldn't live a month, and you know it."

"Why not?"

"Why not?" Hogan echoed angrily. "Mac, you may hate him but not everybody does. He's got a thousand friends in this country—not people like you and me, but poor people, small ranchers, Mexicans, squatters, sheep herders. Half the money he's stolen he's given away to people who need it. I kill him and I buy me a slug in the back." He paused. "Besides it can't be done."

Mac said coldly, "You talk like a damned fool, Frank. Do you think he's immortal? Don't you think lead will make a hole in him? Do you think he can't be killed?"

"How many men have tried it? Where are they now?"

Mac glared at him in speechless impotence, then said, "All right. We'll let the courts kill him. Between six sheriffs in this country, I could get enough on him to hang him twenty-four times."

"You can always try," Hogan said. "But he'll be out. And when he comes back, watch out!"

"Watch out!" Mac thundered, crashing his fist down on the table. "What do you think I've been doing? Do you think I've drawn a free breath for seven years? He could have killed me fifty times, and every time I thought he was going to. I'm living by his pardon, do you understand? He let's me live, gives me my life! Do you think anything could be worse than that—even dying!" He rose now and paced across the room. "Go get your men. I want five men outside the back door of the saloon. I want another five inside the back door. I want three at the livery stable. I'll take six of my own men for the front door, three inside, three outside. If there are any side windows in the Maricopa, I want a man at each. I want every man to carry a shotgun and a six-gun. You'll make the arrest. I'll be with you."

"What charge?" Hogan asked resignedly.

Mac thought a moment. "Let's see. He drove a hundred head of my registered she-stuff out of the corral at the home ranch one day and sold them in town here. Said he was broke. Will that do?"

"Not to hang him with in court."

"He gunned three of my men over in a San Jons salt lick one morning."

"Listen, Mac," Hogan said. "They were gunnies. They were bounty hunting. That won't stick."

"All right. He's got that seven-year-old murder of a nester against him. What about that?"

"If I was you," Hogan said warningly, "I'd try and forget that. That's what started all this, accordin' to report."

"It'll do to finish it with, too," Mac said grimly. "Now, go get your men. When you've rounded them up and placed them, come over to the Ocotillo."

As he was about to step out Hogan touched his arm. "Listen, Mac. There are strangers here in town. If you aim to try and gun him, make it look good."

"I own this town," McCandless replied coldly. "I'll crucify him if I want."

"You may own it, but you don't own men's mouths. If a stranger rides out of here with the news that I framed a killing on St. Vrain, you'll be huntin' a new sheriff—and it won't be blackmail that'll drive me off."

Mac said nothing as they both went out, crossing the street to the Ocotillo, Hogan going into the business houses.

Mac's men, in a back room of the Ocotillo, listened to his plan with misgivings. Superstition or not, they were sure the man or men didn't live yet that could take Poco St. Vrain if he didn't want to be taken. If they killed him, it would mean leaving the country and a good job.

"And if you don't take him, it'll mean the same thing," Mac countered with cold logic. "Either throw in with this scheme, or go to the bank with me and I'll give you your time."

The men looked at each other, and finally the boldest said, "You can give me my time, Mac. I'd rather be out of work and alive than have a job and dead."

"Every man that takes his time today will be mentioned in a reward poster inside the month," Mac said quietly. "Now who's asking for his time?"

Blackmail was one of the handiest tools McCandless used, a tool that was always effective because he hired no riders who couldn't be blackmailed. It worked this time. Sullen and unwilling, the men gave their consent.

CHAPTER ELEVEN

WHEN POCO ENTERED the Maricopa there was a scattering of men at the gaming tables, three or four at the bar, a half dozen or so drinking at tables with the dance-hall girls. He strolled to the bar, ordered a beer, and was consuming it when he felt a pair of arms circle his neck.

He whirled, stepping sideways, his hand on his gun and then saw—and grinned. Standing before him was a slight girl, dark as an Italian, with a wide happy smile on her face that somehow seemed to cancel all the tawdry and cheap finery of her low-cut purple dress.

"Poco!" she cried, and was in his arms, kissing him, hugging him.

"Take it easy, Steamboat," he drawled. "They got bedrooms for that." He untwined her arms from his neck.

"I have one. Will you come up?" Steamboat answered, and grinned.

Poco looked at her fondly. "Still in the sideshow, huh? How long you been here?"

"Buy me a drink and I'll tell you."

Poco said to the bartender, "A gag and a beer, and make the gag real. This is a celebration."

The bartender grinned and nodded and Poco went to a table with the girl. When they were seated, Steamboat pulled her chair close to his, ran an arm through his, and said, "First, will you marry me?"

"Huh-uh."

Steamboat sighed in mock seriousness, but all the time she was looking at him, feasting her eyes on him. "That's what I thought. Dammit. When will you?"

Poco ignored this. "What're you doing here, Steamboat? I left you in Nogales."

"That's the trouble, you left me," Steamboat sighed.

Poco smiled crookedly at her. The drinks came and Steamboat took the whisky. "I haven't touched it since you told me to lay off."

"Good. Touch it now. You don't see the old man often."

"How about yourself? Is beer a celebrating drink?"

Poco's face shadowed a little. "No, some other time."

Steamboat laid her untouched drink on the table. "Trouble coming?"

Poco shook his head and raised his beer to her and drank. "No trouble," he said slowly. "Just a nuisance."

"Fight?"

"I doubt it."

"A woman, isn't it?" Steamboat said, looking him levelly in the eye.

"Sure," Poco agreed readily. "It's always a woman."

"Does she like you?"

"She'd like to poison me," Poco said quietly.

Steamboat nodded wisely. "Then it's love. Oh, dammit, Poco, I knew it! If I was a lady and pretended you were coarse, would you love me?"

"You are a roughneck," Poco told her.

"Are you going to marry her?"

"Not if I can help it."

"You will if she can." She raised a hand to stop any objections he might make. "Don't tell me, Poco. I've never seen the woman yet that wouldn't break a leg to be near you."

"I can show you one," Poco said softly, dreamily, and then his eyes hardened. "The only reason she'd break a leg to be near me is because she thought she could break both mine doing it."

"Do you love her?"

Poco drew marks on the table with the water from the glass bottom. "Love her?" he drawled slowly. "Why, I love you, Steamboat."

"Do you love her?" Steamboat persisted.

Poco looked up at her. "No," he said coldly. "I made her a promise once, because I got her in a jam. I'm keeping my word."

A man entered the saloon then, one of McCandless's men. He looked around, saw Poco, then ordered a drink at the bar.

Poco turned to Steamboat. "I've got to go."

"Already? Please don't."

"Sit tight," Poco said softly, and rose. He strolled up to the head of the room, pausing at a greenfelted poker table at which a houseman and a stranger were matching half dollars and cutting cards straight through the deck.

"That's a game," Poco said. "Is it open?"

The stranger looked up at him. He was a solid middle-aged man, dressed in worn and clean Levis and blue shirt. Poco liked his face. It was reserved, thoughtful, plain, and there was a gleam of humor in his eyes. He gestured to a chair and said, "Sit down."

The stranger removed his Stetson from a chair and covered his untidy mass of tow-colored hair with it.

When another McCandless man came in Poco saw him too. He watched covertly while the second man joined the first at the bar. They talked a moment after which the second puncher looked around the room. He saw Poco and his gaze shifted. Poco was sure of it now. Both were McCandless's men. Turning to flick his cigarette into a spittoon he looked down the long room, over the empty gaming tables and the dance floor to the back door, and he saw three other men seated at a rear table. They avoided looking at him, and they had the sallow appearance of townsmen. He knew what was afoot. The third McCandless man he missed, the fourth he noted idly.

Hogan, the sheriff, came in next. Poco took one look at him and asked the houseman, "That the law?"

The houseman looked and said it was. The stranger

nodded too. When McCandless came in and walked up to the bar, Poco tilted back in his chair and jingled the stack of half dollars in his hand.

"Mac."

McCandless turned.

"Get out!" Poco drawled.

McCandless looked at the sheriff and nodded. The sheriff turned and started over to Poco and Poco slid out of his chair. "Stand still, Lawman," Poco said softly, and Hogan stopped in his tracks.

Poco spoke to Mac. "I know what this is, Mac. Get out!"

The four McCandless hands, their backs to the bar, did not make a move for a gun. McCandless glared at them.

"I won't say it again," Poco said levelly. "I don't want you around. You stink."

Nobody made a move for a gun. Out of the silence somebody from behind Poco said in a tight voice, "Put up your hands, St. Vrain."

Poco ignored him, did not even turn. He was staring at McCandless. For a long moment their glances locked, and then, cursing under his breath, his face black with anger, McCandless turned and went out.

Poco's mild gaze settled on Hogan. "This an arrest, Lawman?" Hogan nodded. "Do you need an army to tell it to me?" Poco asked him. "What's the charge?"

"That seven-year-old murder," Hogan said huskily, wetting his lips. "Understand, St. Vrain, I didn't have nothing to do with this. I'm only an agent of the taxpayers."

"Taxpayer," Poco corrected mildly. He glanced over the McCandless men, who had their hands ostentatiously away from their guns. Then he turned around to look at the men behind him. There were five of them, all holding shotguns trained on him, all townsmen, all nervous.

"You—you give up?" Hogan asked.

Poco yawned. He needed some sleep. "Sure, I give up."

Hogan said to the houseman. "Fisher, get his gun."

"Go to hell," Fisher said, backing against the wall.

"You, stranger," Hogan said. "Flip it out on the table."

"This is your party," the stranger drawled, smiling.

Hogan's face was set and white. "All right, St. Vrain. Take your gun out and lay it on the table. Remember, I never drew a gun on you. I'm just asking you to."

Poco sneered. He flipped out his gun on the table. Hogan, when Poco walked up to him, was braver now.

"Raise your hands, St. Vrain, I'm going to search you for hideouts."

"Take it easy," Poco told him. "I'm ticklish."

Hogan slapped his hip pockets, his shirt pockets, felt his sleeves, felt his waist and his thighs. Satisfied, he said, "Give me your word you won't make a break for it and I won't put the cuffs on you."

"Sure," Poco said, and he put his hands down. He walked past the bar and stepped through the door ahead of the sheriff. Out in the bright glare of the still afternoon, McCandless stood alone in the middle of the road, his legs spread a little, facing the saloon.

Poco slowed down, then stopped, McCandless's waiting immobility a kind of warning to him. Hogan came up beside him and stopped too, eyeing McCandless.

"Get out of the way, Hogan," McCandless said, his voice carrying sharp and flat in that quietness.

For perhaps a second, Hogan stood there, and then he took a step backward. Without turning, Poco reached down and got Hogan's wrist and hauled him up beside him again.

McCandless ignored Hogan now; the warning had been given. He said to Poco, "Now, beg, St. Vrain."

Poco laughed. It was a soft, warm chuckle, barely audible in that hanging silence, but it carried an undertone of jeering amusement and mockery as it died.

"All right," Big Abe said huskily.

"You'll get hurt," Poco warned him quickly, but Big Abe's elbow was already brushing his coat open so he could reach his gun. And Poco, too, was already moving.

He was standing beside Hogan, shoulder to shoulder, and his right hand streaked down, fingers twisted outwards. From Hogan's own hip and holster there was a shuttling sunflash and Poco had the gun out, up, and was already stepping forward as his elbow locked, half-crooked, and the gun roared. McCandless's gun, half-drawn, blasted out through the bottom of the holster. He whirled half around and stepped back to steady himself, surprise washing out the anger in his face.

Poco said, "Don't make me do it again, Abe."

McCandless's hand fell away from his gun butt, and he brought his other hand across his chest to his shoulder, and held it there. On the inside of his gun hand, a trickle of blood traveled down his wrist, across the open palm, down his finger, hesitated, then dropped into the dust.

Poco said, "I told you," and held the gun out to Hogan.

"He's not hurt," Poco said. "Let's go."

Now people were beginning to leave the doorways of the stores hurrying towards McCandless, and Poco said, "All right. Let's go."

On the walk up to the sheriff's office Hogan kept looking at Poco and then at the walk again, about to say something, then checking himself.

Once inside the cell block, he opened a cell door and stood aside.

Poco looked in and shook his head. "Give me one with a window on the street."

Hogan opened another and Poco walked inside. The cot looked comfortable.

"I'd like a beer," he said to Hogan.

Hogan cleared his throat. "Listen, St. Vrain. This won't be for long. McCandless will listen. He's got to."

"The beer," Poco said, yawning. In his haste to leave, Hogan forgot to take his keys. They dangled on a ring from the lock, jingling a little as their swing faded and died. Poco looked at them and then stretched out on the cot. Here, he believed, a man could sleep undisturbed.

CHAPTER TWELVE

"Yessir. I can't help thinkin' I've seen you before. I wish I could remember where," the sergeant said in a conversational musing tone, eyeing Two-Way with something a little less than suspicion.

Two-Way had heard this at hour intervals for two days now, a sort of refrain that had at first chilled him, then amused him, and now bored him, for the sergeant in command of the detail which was escorting them to Rincon was the same sergeant who had interrupted his conversation with Poco in Christian City.

If possible, Two-Way was more shabby looking than the night he appeared at Fort Benjamin. Compared with the eight neat blue-uniformed soldiers who, along with the sergeant, constituted their escort, Cardowan and Two-Way looked shabbier than cast-off hats. There was an easy feeling of comaraderie between Two-Way and the soldiers. He had regaled them with the details of how he and his partner had struck it rich up in the mountains, inventing a story full of romance, daring and luck.

Cardowan, however, had never been wholly at ease since they put foot inside Fort Benjamin. He had expected that at least one of the gang would somehow get word of their true identities to the major or to the pursuing lieutenant. Almost certainly, he thought, one of them would spot the detail and parlay with the sergeant. Two-Way, however, was confident that the leaderless gang, sharing in the guilt of the theft, would not risk brazening it out with the army, since the army would turn the informer over to the civil authorities along with them. And he had been right.

Nevertheless, Cardowan had tried to stem Two-Way's endless flood of chatter to the sergeant, but he had not succeeded. He settled into a surly silence and the soldiers had learned to let him alone.

The cavalcade had come down out of the mountains that morning, and were riding through the foothills now. Two-Way reckoned they were not more than an hour from Rincon. It was time to speak what was on his mind.

He began on Sergeant Rourke.

"That major of yours over yonder is a white man, all right. He don't mind breakin' rules to help a man."

"He's all right," Rourke agreed, "but he don't break rules. He's got them regulations memorized and he runs things by 'em, make no mistake."

Two-Way looked mildly surprised. "You mean, he never broke a rule by sendin' you men to guard us?"

"Nah," Rourke said. "That's what the army's for out here—to look after property and people and bring some kind of order. He can use his own judgment about things like this."

"But you men catch it when you use yours. Is that it?"

"Our what?"

"Judgment."

Rourke spat abstractedly, and turned the question over in his mind. "No, I wouldn't say that. We carry out orders, but it don't matter how very much."

"For instance," Two-Way said, "you mean to say that you could go against orders in this case? The major said to escort me and my partner to Rincon. What if that wasn't very smart?"

"Why ain't it?"

Two-Way pretended to think a minute. "Why, if we was to ride into Rincon with eight soldiers guardin' us, every one would know we had somethin' valuable in them packs. Soon's you soldiers leave, they'd start snoopin'. And as soon as they were sure it was gold, they'd cut our throats in a minute."

Rourke looked at him, scowling.

"But if we was to drift in alone," Two-Way continued, "they'd put us down for a couple of mountain bums and never give us a thought. Ain't that right?"

"Danged if it ain't," Rourke agreed.

"Then how about it?" Two-Way said frankly, and he smiled that disarming smile. "You turn back now and we wander into town alone. If the major asks you about it, tell him we asked to go in alone."

Rourke pulled his horse up and the rest followed suit. They gathered around him while he told them of Two-Way's proposition. "The way I figure it," Rourke finished, "Carlyle wanted us to leave these two men in safe country and see 'em to where they wanted to go. It'd be a sight safer to leave them go into town by theirselves."

The soldiers agreed with their sergeant, who would have done it anyway, but who wanted to appear democratic and seek their counsel.

Two-Way, before leavetaking, brought out a handful of money and tendered it to Rourke, who shook his head. "We're paid by Uncle Sam, mister," he said gravely.

Two-Way smiled. "Sure. This is no bribe. Besides, Uncle Sam don't buy you all the cigars you want. Take it. If you won't keep it for yourselves, turn it over to the company mess for a feed."

When it was put this way, Rourke could hardly refuse. Two-Way thanked them, Cardowan seconding him. They shook hands all around, and the detail started back.

Two-Way eyed them until they were out of sight, then he turned to Cardowan and said in a mock drawl, "Wal, podner, we're on the other side of the mountains. Not bad, huh?"

Cardowan looked around him uneasily at the serrated line of hills stretching to all sides of him. "Let's high-tail it," he said curtly.

"Right," Two-Way agreed. "Anyone know you in Rincon?"

"I been through it, never stayed. Anybody know you?"

"I doubt it. I had a little trouble here ten years ago, but ten years ago I didn't look like this."

On their way into town they decided on their next move. They would drift into the livery stable, and while Two-Way was yarning with the stableman Cardowan would rope each *aparejo* into a compact bundle. They would leave them at the stage station, unaddressed, as part of their luggage. Their very weight would tell the curious that they couldn't contain gold. That night, they would board the stage with their luggage and head south, to Mexico eventually. Shayne would take his time getting down off the mountain, and if he sent a man on ahead into town to rustle up horses and wagons, this man would know nothing of what had happened. Kirk, if discovered, would simply be an outlaw who had died in hiding. Rains would wash away all signs of many horses. They were in gravy, once they were clear of this country.

Two-Way fell silent now, thinking, but not putting into words, what would happen when they took the stage out of Rincon. Cardowan would be armed then, and now, since Poco St. Vrain was dead, he would rate as the deadliest gunman at large. Sooner or later, when the chance came, Two-Way knew Cardowan would kill him for the other half of the gold. The thought didn't bother Two-Way much; since Poco was dead, there was no man he really feared.

The secret of long life, he reflected philosophically, is to get there first. He'd get to Cardowan first. But above all things he had to realize that five hundred pounds of anything, gold or rocks, was a weight around a man's neck if he had to travel fast. He'd have to wait for a sure thing, a sure chance of quick and fast escape before he cut loose on Cardowan. And what pleased Two-Way most was that he knew Cardowan had figured it out the same way. Cardowan would have to wait too.

It fell out in Rincon just as Two-Way had foreseen. The livery stable was at the end of the town's main street, and they drifted in without attracting more than a sidelong glance from townsmen.

At the stable Two-Way drew the boy to one side and dickered over the four horses which they wanted to sell before the stage came in that night. Cardowan roped the sacks in two tight compact bundles and shoved them against the wall along with some sacks of feed, then drifted up to listen to Two-Way, who was concluding his bargain.

"Where's the stage station?" Two-Way asked the lad, after the money had been paid.

"They change horses here. Any heavy stuff they'll pick up here. Passengers and luggage at the hotel."

Two-Way said they had two pieces of freight they wanted put aboard that weighed about five hundred pounds.

The youngster shook his head. "They won't take it unless you buy more seat space. You're only allowed a hundred pounds."

Two-Way told him he'd see about it. At the hotel, Two-Way learned that several people were expected to arrive in Rincon on the evening stage and no seats were sold yet for the trip south. Two-Way breathed a sigh of relief and paid for six places, explaining he had some heavy luggage. The agent, who was the hotel clerk too, told him that he was lucky to find the stage empty. If anyone on it was going on, however, they were entitled to hold their seats.

Stepping out into the street, Two-Way saw it was dusk.

"Guns," Cardowan said.

They crossed to the hardware store. Cardowan spent a good half-hour buying and testing a pair of matched, cedar-handled .45's, while Two-Way looked on, content with a single .38 Smith and Wesson which he rammed in his belt.

Outside again they went into the nearest café, ate, and then sought the street again.

Idling down the walk opposite the jail, picking his teeth, Two-Way noticed the moving light in the jail window opposite. He saw a head framed in it turn away and disappear. He spat, eyeing the jail and the sheriff's office with the gaze of a connoisseur. "That'd be an easy *jusgado* to bust," he said critically.

"They all are," Cardowan replied, not even looking at it. Then he added, "I'd like a drink."

"And I'd like a couple of hands of poker," Two-Way said, indicating the Maricopa, which was just now being lighted up. "We've got an hour yet before the stage."

On the far sidewalk Two-Way suddenly halted, turned and surveyed his partner. "I've heard how you get drunk."

"Yeah," Cardowan said truculently, "and I've heard how you gamble. There's generally a gun fight."

"That's right," Two-Way said amicably. "That's why we'll change our appetites. We've got too nice a stake waiting to risk it by being arrested for making a fight. You gamble and I'll drink. I don't want to drink and you don't want to gamble, so we shouldn't get in trouble."

In the Maricopa, which was just beginning to fill with the after-dinner crowd, Cardowan sought a poker table while Two-Way went up to the bar. In a minute Two-Way was thick in friendly conversation with the barkeep and a quiet-faced tow-headed stranger who was sipping beer and looking thoughtful about it.

Two-Way bought the barkeep a cigar, the thoughtful man another beer, and asked how things were going here.

"I wouldn't know," the stranger said. "I'm new here."

Two-Way downed a slug of bourbon and told the man he was too, that he had just got down from the San Jons yesterday, and that he was fed up with that rock pile to the east forever and a day.

"Prospectin'," the barkeep said, and nodded wisely.

"Not prospecting. Just washing a whole damned peak through my pan while my partner took a whole mountain apart and broke it up."

It was no new thing for a prospector to be garrulous, and Two-Way knew it; moreover, he wanted to establish the fact that he was almost broke, sick and disgusted with the whole business.

Two-Way smiled wryly. "I've worked there with my partner for more'n a month, following the thaw up the slope. An hour ago I shoved in all my dust and seven dollars more for a seat on the stage south. I ain't lucky."

They both laughed in sympathy.

"You didn't run into a couple of men traveling the slope of the San Jons, did you?" the thoughtful man asked.

"A couple of punchers now and then," Two-Way said cautiously. "Always the same ones, though."

"That wouldn't be them. These men would just be passing through and back."

Two-Way studied his drink in silence.

"I was working this slope," he said idly. "Maybe they traveled the other."

"It would be the other," the thoughtful man said.

"Wait a minute," Two-Way said suddenly, frowning. "We passed a couple of riders camped just off the stage road about daylight this morning. I remember because we borrowed some tobacco from them." He looked at the thoughtful man. "What'd they look like?"

"Both younger'n me. One red-headed, answered to the name of Herb. The other was shorter, kind of dude-lookin', but that's just to fool you."

Two-Way felt his pulse quicken; he shook his head.

"No, these were two old gents with a raggedy outfit packed on two burros. It couldn't be your men." He cuffed off his drink and asked indifferently, "Lookin' to meet them?"

The man nodded. "I have been for some time."

Two-Way tasted the excitement in his blood, and smiled at it. This man was evidently sent out by the insurance company as another guard for the gold, another man in an elaborate plan to bring the shipment through in safety. Obviously he hadn't heard of the deaths of the other guards. That wasn't strange since their papers had been stolen and they had probably remained unidentified. Well, there was no reason to get excited just because the gold was right under the man's nose. There was also no reason to tell Cardowan and take the chance of his getting panicky. He felt the false courage that liquor gives, but he did not make the mistake of overestimating it. He changed the subject, and took a cigar himself.

CHAPTER THIRTEEN

S HERIFF HOGAN stayed with McCandless in the hotel room to which he had been taken after the doctor left. McCandless was stretched out on the bed, his coat off, his bloody shirtsleeve cut away and his upper arm bandaged.

Hogan threw him a handful of matches, set the bottle of whisky on the floor, and settled back into the chair which stood beside the table where the lamp sat. He watched McCandless uneasily.

"You say he's in jail," McCandless said.

"Asleep."

McCandless cursed around the stinking four inches of

his cigar. "Well, get it over with. I'm not fooling, Frank."

Hogan said with a show of spirit, "You're more than a mean man, Mac. He could have killed you out there. He even warned you first."

Mac ignored the accusation by saying emphatically, "He *will* kill me. He's promised me that. The thing to do is to get him now, while he's asleep."

"And when it gets out, what then?"

"To hell with what people say!" McCandless said savagely. "It's me or him, and this is the only chance."

Hogan studied the opposite wall, stroking his long line of jaw. He could have told McCandless that Poco would be the winner in this affair. In jail or out, St. Vrain would win. And it was stark fear of him that gave Hogan the courage to shake his head now and say staunchly:

"It's no good, Mac. Count me out."

Mac said, "Do I have to tell you again you'll do it?"

"You don't have to," Hogan said calmly. "I can take a whipping as good as the next man."

"It won't be a whipping, Frank, it'll be a hanging."

"I've got a chance to fight that. I haven't got any chance if I go in there and cut down St. Vrain. I've told you all this before."

Angry impotence was written all over McCandless's rough features, and seeing it, Hogan for once viewed this sensibly. McCandless needed him, and would continue to need him, and while Mac was vindictive, Hogan doubted if his vindictiveness would go to such extreme lengths as his threats.

"Then get somebody that will do it," McCandless ordered.

Hogan leaned forward. "You were shot at one o'clock. Where do you think I was between the time I left St. Vrain to come over here and now?" He leaned back again. "I tell you I've talked to every man in this town that I've got anything on, or who would be likely to do it for money. They say what I say. Life's a little too sweet."

"Everybody?"

"Everybody."

McCandless thought a moment. "What about a stranger, a man who doesn't know St. Vrain and who isn't known here? He could ride away with a pocket full of gold."

Hogan turned this over in his mind. If he could do that, he would still be theoretically blameless for the attempt on St. Vrain's life, and still he would stand in Mc-Candless's good graces. He said, "It might be done."

"Why not? Go round up some hard-case or saddle-bum and find out if he knows much about St. Vrain. If he doesn't, give him a gun and let him in the cell block. Pay any amount of money he wants. If he only wounds St. Vrain, then you shoot him. If he kills him, let him go."

"With the money?"

McCandless said coldly, "That's the kind of bargain I keep, Frank. Yes. With the money."

Hogan rose and left. Going downstairs and crossing the lighted lobby, he tried to recall all the strangers who were in town now. Immediately he thought of the thoughtful quiet-faced man who had been gambling with Poco that afternoon. This man could go into the cell block without alarming St. Vrain. Hogan, crossing the street to the Maricopa, tried to recall the man's face. He looked trustworthy, he remembered, and therefore probably wasn't. The man wore clean clothes. All the more reason for thinking he was likely a bum trying to put up a front for a soft job.

Hogan shouldered through the swing doors and saw the thoughtful stranger talking to a ragged and down-at-the-heels prospector. There was a space between the man and his neighbor to the right and Hogan headed for it.

Two-Way, glancing at the door, saw the sheriff enter. Rather than risk being identified as the gambler who was run out of this town almost a decade ago, Two-Way turned and strolled over to watch Cardowan.

Hogan came up to the bar and ordered a drink. When the thoughtful man nodded recognition, Hogan said, "You're the man who wouldn't take St. Vrain's gun away from him, aren't you?"

The man nodded.

"Said it was my party," Hogan continued, and then

smiled. "Well, it sure enough turned out not to be mine."
He bought the thoughtful man a drink, had one brought
him in return, and then discussed the notorious charac-
ter, Poco St. Vrain, in no mild terms. The thoughtful man
was attentive, nodded, and said nothing.

Hogan felt he was getting nowhere, and besides, this
was too public for the kind of proposition he was con-
templating.

"Yessir," he said reflectively, "that *hombre* has got more
notches on his gun than I'd ever want to answer for."

"That so?" the thoughtful man said non-committally.

Hogan nodded. "Speaking of notches on a gun, what's
the most you ever saw?"

The thoughtful man said he didn't know, and sipped
his beer. "I don't have much occasion to run into gun-
notchers," he offered by way of explanation.

"Well, sir, if you come down to my office, I'll show you
a gun I took from an outlaw here a couple of years back.
I'll give you the rest of the night to count the notches."
He laughed, and added, "Like to see it?"

The thoughtful man said he would. They went out together and up the street. The sheriff's office had a light
burning low in it, and Hogan crossed the room immediately and turned the wick up, saying, "Sit down," to the
thoughtful man, who obeyed. Hogan sat down at the
table.

"I wonder if I got you wrong?" Hogan began suddenly.
"Have I, Mr.—"

"Vanwolkendiefendorfer," the thoughtful man said,
with an utterly sober face.

Hogan stared at him. "What?"

"Vanwolkendiefendorfer," the thoughtful man said,

Hogan leaned back in his chair and said, "Ah," slowly,
as he smiled. "I guess I haven't got you wrong. Not with
that name, anyway."

The thoughtful man might have pointed out that he
was called by, and signed his name, Samuel Van, a con-
cession to the western reluctance to pronounce a name
handed down from revolutionary times by an emigrant

ancestor. He did not, however; it didn't seem necessary. He only nodded agreeably, and sat there with blank eyes.

"Not with that name," Hogan repeated. "No, sir, it's just as plain as if you called yourself Smith or Jones. It's a hell of a handle to hide behind. Is it because a man who's on the dodge needs a name that nobody will remember or can remember? They wouldn't remember Smith and they couldn't remember Vander—whatever the hell it is."

Van nodded gravely.

Hogan was expanding now. He folded his hands behind his head.

"How well do you know this Poco St. Vrain?"

"Cut cards with him," Van said. "Heard the name mentioned, that's all."

"How?"

"Wanted," Van said briefly.

Hogan peered down his nose at him. This was going along as he hoped it would. He shifted his tack. "You waitin' for somebody here?"

Van said he was. He said it slowly, so that it left room for doubt.

"Need money?" Hogan continued.

"Who doesn't?"

"Want to earn some? Not only a lot of money to begin with, but say four thousand collectable in a year or so?"

"How much is a lot?" Van said cautiously.

"Oh, say ten thousand."

Van's face did not change. "Sure. I'd like to earn it. Doing what?"

"Wiping out a killer, a rustler, a thief, a stage robber, bank robber, mine robber, doublecrosser and just a plain poison mean man."

Van's face did not change, and Hogan took silence to mean consent. He swung his chair down and laid his hands on the table. "Understand, there's no risk. You just go in that cell block there with a gun. He's in there, unarmed. You cut down on him. Then I'll pay you, and you jump the country. I'll throw a posse out the other way for you, so you'll have time to ride free." He paused.

"Why don't you do this?" Van asked pleasantly.

Hogan shrugged. "I live here—got to live here. If I did it and a friend of his rode up here to settle, I couldn't do much, could I? No, I need a man that's a stranger, and that wants some quick and easy money."

Van leaned back in his chair now and regarded Hogan much as he would have regarded a piece of corruption he was about to step over.

He only said, "No," very politely, very distinctly, very firmly.

Hogan understood, understood in one half-second that he had made a mistake, that he had talked himself into a jam that he couldn't talk himself out of. But he was not a fool in everything. He pretended he thought Van was after more money.

"All right, all right," he said amicably, tilting his chair back and dragging his hands off the table, so they fell on his thighs, "we'll make it twelve thousand."

Van said, "No."

Hogan said, "Fifteen, then," and settled his chair down on all four legs. Under the table he drew his gun and leveled it at Van.

"No," Van said.

Hogan smiled narrowly. In the silence that followed, the click of his cocking gun was plain. Van glanced down, could not see the gun, but understood the sound. He said calmly, "There's not much to say. If I said yes, you wouldn't believe me now, would you?"

Hogan said coldly, "Pull down that front shade."

Van, after a second's pause, rose.

"You make a move for that gun of yours and I'll do it in public and have proof you drew first."

Van pulled down the shade to the front window.

"Get over against that side wall," Hogan ordered. He brought the gun above the table level now.

Van, his face thoughtful, a bit scornful, moved over.

"I'd hate to stick my head in the noose you're sticking yours into," Van said. "I represent—"

"A man with guts," a quiet, cold voice finished from

the cell block door.

Hogan whirled, his gun waist high, to confront the steady black barrel of the Colt in Poco St. Vrain's hands.

Poco said coldly, "You've got it out, whippoorwill. Shoot."

Hogan dropped the gun as if it were red-hot. Luckily the jar on the floor did not send it off.

Poco shut the door behind him and leaned against it, regarding Hogan with cold, predatory eyes, his lip lifted in a sneer. Hogan backed off, his face going ashen.

Poco's gaze shuttled to Van, who was unbuckling his shell belts with a kind of thoughtful unhaste, and he laid them on the table along with his hat. Then he lifted the table into a corner, slid the chairs under it, locked the front door, and walked out into the middle of the room. Poco smiled crookedly and said nothing.

"Come over here," Van said gently to Hogan.

Hogan knew what was up. He flattened against the wall and held his breath. Van walked over to him in three long strides, grasped him at the V of his vest, whirled him away from the wall in a dizzy half circle which he completed by driving a thick fist into Hogan's face. Hogan back-pedaled halfway across the room, fell on his back and skidded the rest of the way to the wall.

Van said gently, "Do I have to kick you up or will you get up?"

Hogan knew misery when he saw it, and like any man he preferred to fight it. He rose and waited for Van, crouched a little, spitting blood, his guard up. Van walked across the room and when he reached Hogan, Poco never quite understood how it happened. It was as if Hogan had no arms, or no arms that could move. Without pausing in his stride Van drove his thick arm through Hogan's guard into his face again, and Hogan's head snapped back against the wall. Moreover, it kept snapping back and forward, with a degree less resilience than a punching bag. When Hogan's knees began to buckle, Van braced them with his own leg, grasped Hogan by the shirt front, lifted him off the floor, turned around and stood him up clear of the wall. Then gently, patiently, he slapped the sheriff's face until the eyes began to focus again.

"Stand up," he said quietly, and took his hand away. Hogan tottered and Van grabbed him again, slapped him again.

Then he took his hand away. Hogan stood swaying, but he was rooted to the spot.

"Put up your hands," Van said gently.

Hogan did. And then Poco began to understand how a man can have the life in him beat so low that he can never fully regain it again. Hogan fought. He fought with the maniacal fury of a cornered animal, while Van, not breathing hard, did not move out of his tracks. Van stood there, bent over a little, his thick chunky arms up. Every one of Hogan's wild swings he chopped short and down with solid ungiving ax strokes, and each time he did it, he drove those same short and ponderous blows into Hogan's body. It was mechanical, merciless. Van did not try to knock him down, or hit him hard enough to numb the senses. He simply whittled away, dealing out a full measure of pain, of broken ribs, of ripped skin. Every time Hogan, slacked off in weariness, some knifing hurt would rouse him to madness again.

And then, as if the cruelty of this was too revolting to behold any longer, Van stepped in with one long stride, the muscles on his left shoulder coiling as his thick fist looped up to Hogan's shelving chin. Hogan, arms down, toppled over and lay on his back without moving.

"I guess I've got some Indian in me," Van said, and added softly, "But, damn! I hate a killer that's a coward too."

Poco said, "I heard him."

Van was unmarked except for a pair of raw knuckles. Hogan's face was a meaty, bloody pulp, the nose mashed in, the mouth shapeless, even the glazed eyes bleeding at the corners.

"Put him in the cell block," Poco said. "Then you better high-tail it. I'll take the blame for this, but you better not get caught here."

Van looked up quickly. "You will not," he said flatly, firmly. "I don't know if you just walk through jail bars, but I do know you walked through those in time to save my life. Be damned if I'll let you do it again."

"But they'll hang your hide on the fence, fella. They're afraid of me."

"I don't pay back a favor by accepting another," Van said, smiling a little. "Open the door."

Poco shrugged and opened the corridor door while Van picked Hogan up and took him into the cell Poco had just left. The door was open, unlocked, a matter of precaution Poco had seen to that afternoon when the keys were left in the lock by Hogan.

In the office again, Van strapped on his guns, turned down the light, raised the shade and unlocked the door. Poco walked through onto the sidewalk and stopped. He said idly over his shoulder to Van, "When they see me, there'll be a commotion here. You better slip out of town then."

"And let them hang Hogan's beating on you? Huh-uh. I'll stick."

Again Poco looked at him curiously. This was a strange loyalty, and he hardly deserved it. He said, "When I get through what I'm going to do they'll have forgot Hogan. Now high-tail it." He was thinking of Two-Way and Cardowan. They'd be in a saloon, drinking or gambling. Cardowan would be the one to watch. Two-Way would be afraid. He'd no more throw a gun on Poco than he would on a sheriff's posse, and Poco knew it. It was the lean-faced Texas killer that would get it. He heard Van's voice rise and die, and he said, "What?"

"Trouble?" Van repeated.

"Not much."

"I'll side you," Van said quietly. Poco looked at him.

"I don't need help."

"You'll get it, just the same," Van said firmly. "You'll have to make a getaway. I'll cover it."

Poco laughed silently. "Listen," he said. "Do you know who I am?"

"Poco St. Vrain."

"All right. I don't know who you are. But—"

"Sam Van."

"All right, Sam Van. You've got a life ahead of you and it won't be on the dodge. When I walk into the Maricopa Saloon, or the Ocotillo, I'm going to kill two men. Nobody will make a move until I get out of town. I can take care of myself. Why should I toll you in on it? It's no business of yours. The killings won't help you. The—"

"Will they help you?" Van said quietly.

Poco paused, and looked at his companion a little more shrewdly. The street was dark except for the lights from the stores, and Poco wondered if he had misjudged his man. He said, "You couldn't be a preacher, could you?"

"I didn't mean that," Van said sturdily. "I mean, will these two killings help you? Have you got to do them?"

"Well, now," Poco drawled, "somebody has. They're both rats. No, one's a rat and a backshooter, and the other's just a poison, blood-loving killer."

"What did they do to you?"

Poco's manner changed imperceptibly. He said quietly, "Take it easy, Sam Van. Your nose is getting long."

"Sure," Van said patiently, "but if I help you kill two men, I want to know first if they deserve killing, and second why I'm helping to kill them."

"You aren't."

"I am." And he added with gentle insistence, "What did they do to you?"

Poco knew he should be angry at this man, but the quiet and sturdy way of him, the doglike determination to help and his way of arriving so simply at his own kind of justice gave Poco pause. He said, "They've got something I want that doesn't belong to them, that will bring a lot of misery to innocent people if it isn't returned."

"Then take it. Let them go. Stealing isn't a thing for you to judge, nor me either. Take them to jail and then tell the law."

"I don't fight that way," Poco said coldly.

"Try it once."

"I can't. If I told the law, they'd have me too."

"Write it then. Hogan's down. You've got the cell keys. Throw them in, take the keys and write it on a card and mail it. You'll be out of town."

When Poco said nothing, Van went on, "Son, I'm maybe slow and a little cautious, but I never killed a man yet without I had a good reason. And I never killed a man yet for stealing, because stealing is a mighty human fault. We all do it some time in our lives. You can't kill a man for doing what you've done yourself. You can punish him, but not kill him."

Poco said, "Listen, Grandpa. When I—"

"I know, I know," Van said with a kind of insistent gentleness. "They've got something you want, that you've got to return. All right, you'll get it. Let me handle this. I'll get whatever it is and I'll get it without killing them. And I'll see they get what's coming to them."

"No you won't. You can't. I'm the only man that can give them what's coming to them. Now get out of the way."

"All right," Van said, stepping aside. "Is it the Maricopa?"

Poco said, "You stay here."

"No. I'm siding you."

Poco's patience snapped. His hand fell to the butt of the gun rammed in the waist of his Levis. "I said you stay, Grandpa. Do I have to fix you so you can't come?"

"If you wanted to do that you could have let Hogan cut down on me, St. Vrain. Huh-uh. You aren't a killer. Now go about your bull-headed business. I'm going with you."

They stood there in the near dark, Van's gentle voice fading and dying, but the force of his words and his will as immovable as mountains, his lack of anger, of any desire to use force, and his utter reasonableness was what puzzled Poco and melted his irritation.

He said, "Come along, then. Only don't get in my way."

They approached the Maricopa together. No one was on the sidewalks and the horses at the tie rail were standing in hipshot and sleepy indolence. Far down the street the night stage swung into the light in front of the feed stable and pulled up with a screech of brakes. The noise from the saloon was a little muted here on the street. Poco heard Van say, "You want another gun?"

"One's enough," Poco answered briefly.

Van held out one of his guns. "Ram it alongside that other. You may need it."

Poco accepted it without a word.

"What do these men look like?" Van inquired.

"One's a long, sleepy Texan. His partner is shorter, smooth talking, wears a black moustache. Nice to talk to, but if a man has any sense he'll cover his ears."

"I know," Van said. He remembered the prospector.

At the door Poco hitched up his pants, and said out of the side of his mouth, "Remember, stay clear of me."

And then he shouldered in, Van trailing him. He stood by the door, just so, looking over the crowded, smoke-blued room. He spotted Two-Way's back at the bar, and ignored it. Then he saw Cardowan, back to the sidewall, scowling over a hand of draw poker. Slowly he started walking toward this table. The men at the bar saw him first, and a dead, watchful silence fell on them. Like a wave of muteness it swept down the long room. Men stopped in mid-conversation and turned their heads.

Poco said softly without looking at Two-Way, "I see you, Two-Way," and in that muting hum of talk, Two-Way heard it and stood utterly still.

Now Poco was twenty feet from Cardowan's table. Without knowing why, or by watching the direction in which Poco was looking, men cleared a way for him, leaving their chairs and backing toward the wall.

The man facing the door at Cardowan's table looked up, and over his face washed an expression of haste, only haste. He laid his cards down and slid out of his chair. The other three saw him, looked around, and did the same. Only Cardowan, still scowling over his hand, was oblivious to their departure. Then he heard, sensed, the silence.

He looked up quickly at the room, understood, and just as quickly swiveled his head toward the door.

"Hello, Joker," Poco drawled. He stood motionless,

hands on hips, his arrogant smile jeering and faint.

The color washed out of Cardowan's face toward his neck. His jaw slacked imperceptibly, and he laid both hands on the table to rise. Then he knew that he would never make it, and he settled back in his chair, his tongue moving between his teeth.

"This is blackjack, Joker," Poco drawled. "Cut loose your dogs."

Cardowan sat without moving a muscle, without speaking, with held breath. He sat that way for ten long seconds while the room heard the oblivious tick of the clock behind the bar. Then Cardowan swallowed and shook his head. He shoved his hands farther out on the table and held them there, shaking his head again in silent refusal to meet the challenge.

Then a voice, Van's voice, spoke from behind Poco, "See? You can't cut down on a man who won't fight."

Poco said nothing. Van turned to Two-Way and said, "Come here."

Two-Way walked over, his face stiff with fear. Van took his gun, then stepped around Poco and started toward Cardowan.

"Wait," Poco said.

Van ignored him. He walked behind Cardowan's chair, flipped out his Colts, then stepped back.

"Come along," he said gently.

Cardowan rose.

"Go on out," Van said.

Cardowan started toward the door. Poco half-turned as Cardowan passed and said quietly, "Tinhorn."

Two-Way fell in beside Cardowan and both walked toward the door, Van behind them, Poco behind him. In that same silence, they marched out.

"Upstreet," Van said when they were on the sidewalk.

The driver atop the stage, across the street in front of the hotel, looked down and across at the Maricopa, its quietness puzzling him.

Then his gaze came back to the girl standing on the walk. "They say he's in the Overland House here, Miss," he said. "They told me down at the feed stable he got shot up in a gunfight here this afternoon."

"Bad?"

"I reckon not, Miss. Leastways he's here and you won't have to ride on to the ford and wait for some TC puncher to pick you up."

"Thank you. Good night."

"Good night."

Kate Shayne, dressed in a dark blue traveling suit, walked up the steps to the Overland House, described her bag, which was indeed the only one left standing on the sidewalk, to the clerk, and then, without turning around, without noticing the four men who were walking upstreet in silence, entered the hotel.

The shotgun messenger, who had just walked up from the feed stable and was leaning against the left rear wheel of the stage, rolling a cigarette, said, "She must be a stranger."

"She is. And a plumb tired one too."

"Why?"

"Why she slept right through the change of horses yonder and I had to shout to wake her up here."

"Purty, huh?"

"Plumb bodacious."

The usual crowd which met the stage always gathered at the feed stable so as to get the news first. Only those who were seeing friends off collected at the hotel. There was no one here tonight, but the driver seemed to be waiting for someone.

Presently the middle-aged clerk hobbled out the hotel door and down the steps. "Can't find 'em," he announced.

The driver swore. "We can't wait no longer, Russ."

"I know that," Russ growled. "Go ahead."

The driver motioned with his thumb to the two heavy tarp-wrapped bundles, one laced in the express compartment under the driver's feet, the other in the express compartment over the rear axle. "These belong to 'em?"

"What does it say?"

"No address. It must be theirs."

The driver flipped his cigarette away with a curse. "We got to turn around and take these off again, Russ?"

"Take 'em off here," the guard said. "Let's tote 'em up and Russ can leave word at the feed stable they're up here."

Swearing disgustedly, the driver wound the ribbons around the brake rod and swung down. They took the bulky freight out, and together carried it into the hotel lobby and shoved it under the counter.

"They paid for six places," Russ said thoughtfully. "They'll be sore as hell to miss this. They wanted it bad."

"You got the dinero, why bellyache?" the driver grunted.

"Yeah, Russ. If they don't show up you'll keep it. How about a coupla cigars to help us forget it?"

The clerk, a meek and patently honest man, and a sedentary one in the bargain, was flattered at this intimation that he was capable of being dishonest and cagey enough to hide it in the bargain. He took four cigars out of a box and shoved them across to the two men.

"Get the hell out of here, you pirates," he growled.

They took the cigars, winked solemnly, and departed. Outside he heard the stage pull out and smiled thoughtfully. He liked these hardbitten and profane men who dared a slug of buckshot in the belly every time they left the lights of town. And, he reflected truthfully, you'd hunt a long time before you found a more honest lot of men.

CHAPTER FOURTEEN

Poco lounged against the doorframe of the cell block, building a smoke, while Van rummaged around in the sheriff's desk for the key ring. Finding it, Van came through to unlock a cell and Two-Way and Cardowan stepped inside.

"Leave it open," Poco said, and lounged erect. Van stepped away.

"I've got business," Poco continued. "Mind leaving us?"

Van said he didn't, and walked out, closing the corridor door behind him.

Poco strolled up to the cell door and leaned against it, one hand rammed in his waistband, the other cradling his cigarette. Two-Way was on one cot, Cardowan on the other, and he regarded them with a curious mixture of contempt and pity.

Cardowan kept staring at Poco, wetting his lips, trying to still his shaking hands. He could see the bruises on Poco's hands, the rope burns, but it did not explain a man risen from the dead. Poco only looked at him and smiled.

Two-Way, however, was the first to speak, and he looked at Cardowan while he said to Poco, "Well, Poco. I've been foxed right enough. That yellow belly told me you were dead, pushed off a cliff. I might have known he lied. He had so many men waiting down there in the boulder field that I had to throw in with him to get our half."

Cardowan turned his gaze from Poco to Two-Way. "Go ahead," he drawled. "Tell him why you had so many men down there."

"To keep whippoorwills like you from jumping Poco," Two-Way answered smoothly. "We were partners. I figured I couldn't do any less."

A thin amused smile appeared on Poco's face. Cardowan was less appreciative. He leaned forward, hands on knees, and said slowly, "You lie in your throat, Two-Way. You aimed to jump Poco and me when we came down. You said so."

Two-Way shrugged. "I had to tell you that or you wouldn't have left your back to me for one blind second."

Cardowan leaped to his feet. "You double-crossin' rat! Stand up here."

Two-Way smiled slowly and jerked his head in Poco's direction. "I wouldn't get salty. My partner's here. He's salty too."

Poco said, "I don't see his partner here, Joker. Get on with it."

Two-Way now leaped to his feet, standing on the cot, knowing his bluff was played out. Cardowan rushed him.

Two-Way kicked him hard, the toe of his boot brushing through Cardowan's upthrown arms and cutting his cheek. But the Texan came on, grasped Two-Way's leg and threw him down on the cot. Two-Way fought with the savagery of a cat, clawing, scratching, biting, kicking, and Cardowan had his hands full, so that he could not rightly land a telling blow. They rolled off the cot onto the floor, Cardowan on top. Two-Way got one of Cardowan's hands in his mouth and sunk his teeth in clear to the bone, while Cardowan, his curses almost sobs, slugged at Two-Way's face with the fury pain gives. Poco, aloof, watching it with impersonal boredom, knew what to expect, and it happened. Cardowan's blows, raining on Two-Way's forearm, which was held over his face for protection, were ineffective, and the big Texan knew it. His long, lean fingers sought Two-Way's throat. He writhed with the agony of Two-Way's teeth in his hand, but he put every ounce of his weight and strength into the hand around the gambler's throat. And Two-Way, his face growing from pale to red to purple, bulged the muscles of his jaw with the effort to crunch Cardowan's bones.

Poco lounged over and tapped Cardowan on the shoulder. "Get up," he said.

And Two-Way, his eyes almost popping out of his head, understood that help had come, and he opened his mouth. Cardowan rose, holding his bleeding hand, cursing savagely, while Two-Way lay on his back, breathing in long retching sobs as he fought to get his wind back.

Poco was leaning against the cell door again, faintly smiling. "Sit on the cot," he said.

Again they were facing each other, glaring. Poco dropped his cigarette, placed a foot on it, then said quietly, "Where is it?"

Two-Way and Cardowan looked at each other, each calculating if the other would back him up in a lie, or if not that, how he could betray the other.

Finally Two-Way said to Cardowan, "Let me handle this, *Tejano*. I may make it pay." He looked up at Poco. "If we tell you, what's our cut?"

Poco drawled softly, "Maybe that's funny."

"Maybe it is," Two-Way said, "but here's how it stands. A three-way split or you can whistle for the gold."

"I'll let you walk out of here without taking a gun to you," Poco said slowly. "That's my deal. I get the gold—all of it. You get out without my cutting you to doll rags."

"You won't hurt us," Two-Way drawled. "You can't. We're the only two people that know where that gold is." He smiled affably now, and said, "I think I'll talk to McCandless. Maybe he'll split with us. After all, half is better than nothing to a man with sense."

"You really want to parley with him, do you?" Poco asked politely.

"Unless you start talking sense, Poco. Give us your word that if we take you to the bullion you'll split it three ways and let us ride free. I'd take your word. You've never gone back on it yet. If you won't, then I think we'll just stay here and start yelling for McCandless until they bring him."

It was a shrewd move on Two-Way's part. He knew Poco St. Vrain well enough to be sure he wouldn't kill them both in cold blood. But he didn't know Poco well enough to understand why he turned now, slammed the cell door shut, and walked out.

Cardowan said to Two-Way, "Where's he gone?"

Two-Way shrugged.

"You'll never make it stick."

Two-Way said, "I'll make it stick a little better than your killing him."

Cardowan said sharply, "I tell you I pushed him over that cliff! I heard him scream! I even saw the marks in the snow! Hell, how was I to know he'd come out alive?"

"You should have known you'd never kill him, *Tejano*," Two-Way said slowly. "When he gives up his scalp, it'll be to a better Indian than you are."

In the outer office Van was seated in a chair smoking.

Poco said, "I'll be back in a minute. Don't let anybody talk to them."

He swung out into the night, ducked under the tie

rail and crossed to the hotel. At the desk he asked pleasantly of the clerk. "What number does McCandless have?"

The clerk said, "Doc's orders nobody sees him."

"What number?" Poco asked patiently.

Something about this still-faced, too-polite questioner changed the clerk's mind. He said, "Ten."

Poco thanked him and went upstairs. At number ten he did not even knock, but pushed open the door, striking a match at the same time.

Abe McCandless was dozing in his clothes on the bed. The light was still on. He had gone to sleep waiting for Hogan to return.

Poco shook him and McCandless opened his eyes. For one brief second he gazed sleepily at his awakener, and then he reared up into a sitting position, pushing himself away from Poco.

"Come along," Poco said.

Without asking where or why, McCandless rose and followed Poco out of the room, down the stairs, across the street and into the sheriff's office.

Van nodded to McCandless and said nothing. Poco said to Van, "See that nobody comes in."

He ushered McCandless into the cell block, picked up the lantern, and unlocked the cell where Two-Way and Cardowan were watching in silence.

Poco stepped aside and said to McCandless, "Sit down."

McCandless, looking puzzled, sat on Two-Way's cot, back to the sheriff's cell.

Poco now, under the silent gaze of all of them, made a cigarette, lighted it, and leaned against the doorframe.

"This is your town, isn't it, Mac?" Poco began.

Abe nodded.

"You own the sheriff. Besides owning him, you have about eight men in town now. If you gave the word, you could raise a posse of almost the whole town, couldn't you? If you had an hour, you could bring about twelve more hands from your spread out north, couldn't you?"

Abe nodded again. Two-Way was watching Poco, trying to anticipate what he was about to say, but Poco went on imperturbably.

"Your word is pretty much law here, isn't it, Mac? You'd never let a little thing like a trial stand in the way of a lynching that was due, would you?"

McCandless said deprecatingly, "I wouldn't say that," but his looks, his tone, his manner belied it.

Poco reached in his pocket and brought out the folded sheaf of papers—the insurance man's identification papers, as well as the papers Shayne had signed. He held them up and looked at Two-Way. "Remember when I took these off you?" he asked gently, sardonically. "Joker's got the mates. It's only a short ride to Fort Benjamin, where the army will back up the story about the two pack horses and what they carried." He paused. "McCandless owns this town. You heard him say so."

Two-Way licked his lips. He was sitting on dynamite, and he knew it, for now that Poco had conjured McCandless out of the night, the scheme didn't look so good to Two-Way.

Poco continued, "You know there's two men dead already over this—two men that aren't hard-cases and gunnies, two men that a great big outfit might have valued. Understand what I mean?"

Two-Way nodded briefly, but he was scared.

"It's a lot easier to tell and ride out," Poco drawled.

"I'll make it a fourth," Two-Way said huskily, with just a suggestion of his old confidence. He saw now what a beautiful trap Poco had set for him. McCandless, if he thought Two-Way one of the thieves—and Poco could prove that by the officer at Fort Benjamin, and by Two-Way's presence in Silver City when Jacob Finger was killed—would mete out his own brand of justice, and it would be at the end of a rope, gold or no gold. Poco would keep him locked in here until McCandless verified the facts and raised the lynch mob. McCandless wouldn't bother to bargain. And while Poco was just as guilty, he w s free, not in prison, and he could run.

"A fourth, you say?" Poco drawled. "Too much." He tapped the sheaf of insurance papers. "All right. You make your proposition to McCandless."

McCandless looked from Poco to Two-Way, puzzled. "What is it?"

"Go on," Poco urged sardonically.

Two-Way opened his mouth to speak, then closed it and shook his head.

Poco said, "Then I'll make it for you," and he reached out the insurance papers to McCandless, who put out his hand to take them. Two-Way exploded off the cot and batted the papers to the floor. McCandless looked from Poco to Two-Way and then back to Poco.

Then he leaned over to pick the papers off the floor, just as Two-Way said, "You win, damn your black soul!"

Poco stretched out his foot and put it on the papers just as McCandless touched them.

"Leave them, Mac," Poco said. "You go out in the office for a minute. I may need you again."

McCandless, puzzled at these elaborate and wholly senseless doings, nevertheless rose meekly and went out.

When the corridor door shut, Poco said quietly, "Where is it?"

Two-Way, first cursing, said, "Down in the feed stable alongside—" He ceased talking and his mouth sagged. Then he leaped to his feet. "Great God!" he yelled. "It's gone!"

Poco knew Two-Way well enough to distinguish his sham from the real thing. Cardowan, equally astonished started to curse with slow and vitriolic bitterness.

"The stage!" Two-Way said hoarsely. "Has it gone yet?"

"It was in town before I came into the saloon."

Two-Way sagged onto the cot. "It's there. On the stage. We bought seats on it and arranged to have the stuff loaded at the feed stable. It's on the stage, sure as hell's hot! Oh, damn, damn—" Suddenly he ceased speaking again, and then started to laugh. He laughed long and loud, and turned to Poco, about to speak.

"I wondered when you'd think about it being my gold and not yours," Poco said dryly. He turned and started down the corridor.

"You going to turn us over to McCandless, Poco?" Two-Way wailed.

Poco did not answer. In the office he asked Van one question on his way out.

"Where's your horse and what is it?"

"Rent stall at the feed stable. Roan, branded Cross Hammer."

"Don't let Mac talk to them," Poco said, and went out.

At the feed stable he asked the attendant, "Were you here this afternoon?"

"Sure."

"Did two miners leave some heavy freight here to be loaded on the stage?"

"Sure."

"Was it loaded?"

"Sure."

"You're sure of that?"

"I done it myself," the attendant said.

Poco said, "Saddle up that roan in the rent stall branded Cross Hammer and my horse, too."

Back in the office Poco said to Mac, "You can go, Mac."

McCandless left gladly. Poco searched through the sheriff's desk until he found his gun and belt, and then said, "I had your horse saddled, Sam. You've sided me all night, but now it's time for you to high-tail. When I leave, you'd be a fool to stay."

"Which way you riding?" Van asked.

"South."

"So am I."

"Not with me."

"Why not? We might's well throw in together."

Poco said coldly, "I'm obliged for the lift, Sam. You'll do to ride the river with. But I'm a lonesome man. I like my own company best. So I'm riding south, and I'm riding alone."

Sam shrugged and raised his hand, palm upwards. "*Bueno*. But tell me one thing before you go. What's this all about?"

"No."

Poco smiled, to take the edge off his bluntness, strapped his belt on, and went into the cell block.

Two-Way and Cardowan were holding the bars like two monkeys at a zoo, following him with their eyes. Poco stopped in front of Cardowan, who let his hands fall and backed away.

"You letting us out, Poco?" Two-Way asked.

Poco did not look at him. He was looking at Cardowan instead.

"Joker," he said softly, "I used to think about you once in a while, wondering how I was going to kill you when you finally worked up the whisky guts to face me. I won't again—not from now on. You can't make a man out of a rat, not by putting a pair of pants on him and giving him guns. But get this. I won't hunt you. If you were over the next hill from me and I knew it, I wouldn't take the trouble to ride over and rub out your mark. But if I ever see you again—*if I ever get you within gun range*—I'll tattoo a stripe down your back with slugs and when I get done the color won't be yellow any more."

His gaze shuttled to Two-Way. He raised his hands, snapped his fingers, and with that eloquent, simple and wordless explanation that Two-Way wasn't worth wasting words on, turned and left the cell block.

He tossed the cell keys on the desk and said to Van. "I wouldn't let them out till morning, Sam. Just leave the key on the desk and ride off. *Adios*, friend."

"So long," Van drawled, and watched him go out.

Van sat there, musing, wondering what it was that was causing all this uproar, reflecting that someone, some time, had misinformed him as to Poco St. Vrain. Tough he was, a killer, maybe. But the only killing he seemed anxious to do contributed to the extermination of his own kind.

When he heard the *cloppity-clop* of a horse galloping down the street, he smiled. Maybe St. Vrain was right. Maybe he should clear out of town before someone found Hogan and he talked. He rose and stretched, and looked at the door to the cell block.

Even as he was regarding it with mild curiosity, wondering why St. Vrain wanted these men kept in here, he heard one of them call.

"Come in here a minute, pardner."

CHAPTER FIFTEEN

VAN OPENED THE DOOR and went in, picking up the lantern just inside the door.

Two-Way smiled disarmingly. "You aim to keep us in here long?"

"I'm leaving."

"Let us out."

Van shook his head. "St. Vrain said you'd keep till morning. I reckon you will."

Two-Way turned around and looked at Cardowan. "Hear that, pardner. Is that hard to figure out?"

"Not very," Cardowan said bitterly. He was sitting hunched on the cot, holding his hand.

Two-Way turned to Van again, regarding him with meditative eyes. Then he said, "You're waiting here in Rincon for somebody, aren't you?"

Van said, "I told you I was."

"You want me to tell you who they are?" Two-Way drawled.

"You can always try. But don't take all night."

"Herb Skelton and Jake Finger. Right?"

Van set the lantern on the floor and stared.

Two-Way said, "They were guarding a shipment of gold down from McCandless's mine, weren't they?"

Van nodded mutely, looking from one to the other.

Two Way drawled, "Well, it's gone, pardner. There's no gold and there's no Herb Skelton and no Jake Finger."

"I don't believe it," Van said slowly.

Two-Way turned to Cardowan. "Hand it over, *Tejano*."

The Texan handed over the credentials of the dead agent, and Two-Way watched Van read them. "That," Two-Way announced, "was found in Poco St. Vrain's warbag down at the feed stable when we drifted in this afternoon." His voice lost its drawl suddenly and he said sharply, "Do you want that gold, fella?"

Van was turning to leave when Two-Way said, "Hear it out. Do you want that gold?"

"I'm supposed to see it gets to Phoenix. I want it bad enough to hold a job and feed a family is all," Van said.

"I can take you to it," Two-Way said flatly.

"How?"

"Because I know where it is. I know how I can beat St. Vrain to it."

"What do you get out of this?" Van asked slowly.

Two-Way smiled narrowly. "Just the chance to see Poco St. Vrain cut to doll rags, is all. That's all I want."

Van said, "Yeah?" cynically, and started for the door again.

"You wake the town, fella, and tell them, and you'll play merry hell getting that gold to Phœnix. If you took a posse out, they'd kill you for it as soon as they knew it. Besides, you don't know where it is. Better talk sense."

Van paused, his back to them, then turned around slowly. "You say you know where it is?"

"If I didn't, what's Poco St. Vrain riding hell-for-leather out of town for? Let us out of here and we'll take you to it."

Van recalled the reason Poco gave for wanting to kill these two men, and suddenly he understood how he had been taken in, how Poco had lied to win him over to his side, how what he really wanted was to get these two men out of the way so that he could take the gold. He was riding for it now. To prove it, if these men had stolen it as St. Vrain claimed, why didn't he turn them over to the law? Why didn't he tell McCandless, whose gold it was? Van looked at the pair of them, and he knew they were scum, hard-cases, but he was also a man who believed in himself. He could prod them at the point of a gun as far as across the street to McCandless, who would get men. The time for secrecy was past.

He said, "Wait a minute," and started for the office to get the key.

When he was gone, Two-Way said gloomily, "This is a long shot."

Cardowan said nothing, only reached out for the lantern standing in the corridor, and dragged it to him. Unscrewing the cap of the fuel tank, he raised it to his lips and poured a slug of kerosene into his mouth. Two-Way, watching him, said, "Play it crazy."

The lamp was in the corridor again when Van came back with the key in one hand, a drawn Colt in the other. Cardowan sat hunched over on the cot, holding his hand. When the door swung open, Two-Way had to shake Cardowan by the shoulder to get his attention.

"Come out slow and careful," Van warned. Then, as Two-Way continued to urge Cardowan, who acted sick and listless, Van said, "What's the matter with him?"

Two-Way said with feigned bitterness, "Some more of Poco St. Vrain's work. Torture."

Van said curiously, "Let's see."

Cardowan rose and stumbled out through the cell door. Then he raised his hand, raw and bleeding where Two-Way had bitten him, and held it up for Van to look at.

Van let his gaze fall to the hand, and in that moment Cardowan squirted the kerosene from his mouth square in Van's eyes, dodging aside as he did so. The blast of the gun was immediate, but Van had closed his eyes against the raw smart of the kerosene and in that second Cardowan batted both his arms down to his side. It was Two-Ways rocketing swing that caught Van on the jut of his chin, and he melted to the floor.

Cardowan leaped for the gun in Van's hand, but Two-Way stamped his foot down on it. Then Cardowan dived for the other gun in Van's belt and at the same time Two-Way scooped the gun off the floor. They both came up, guns in hand, cocked, pointing at each other.

Then Two-Way smiled crookedly. "Dead heat, *Tejano*. Put it away. We aren't out of here yet."

"I can wait," Cardowan drawled with deceptive mildness. Watching each other, they both put their guns away. They made quick work of trussing Van and gagging him before they dumped him in the cell.

Out in the office Two-Way placed his hand on the butt of his gun and said, "I'm through being a sucker, *Tejano*. From now on it'll take more than a tinhorn gambler and a yellow-bellied gunman to get Poco St. Vrain."

Cardowan smiled narrowly, his cold eyes unblinking and savage. He raised a hand to the butt of his gun, but Two-Way wasn't to be bluffed.

"Want to make anything out of it?" Two-Way drawled calmly.

Cardowan's eyes narrowed in bewilderment. Most men were afraid of him, afraid of his whims and his threat, but Two-Way was facing him now on even terms and daring him to draw. He wished savagely that Two-Way had not seen Poco make him take water that night.

He said, "Not now, Two-Way. I'll need you before this is over."

"All right. Then get this. I'd rather have a quarter of that gold than none of it. *Sabe?*"

"So would I."

"Good. Then I'm going over to McCandless and spill the story—for one quarter of that gold."

"He'll kill you," Cardowan drawled.

"Not when he hears this yarn. I'll make him think I've been waiting years to do him the favor. Does he know you?"

"He knows my name. Everybody does, but not my face," Cardowan answered arrogantly.

"Then I'll tell him it was you and Poco that took it. You keep your mouth shut, *Tejano,* and we'll pull through this with a poke full of gold. Don't, and—well, you'll miss meeting Poco again." He eyed Cardowan shrewdly. "I need you, yellow belly. I need your guns."

Cardowan retrieved his matched, cedar-handled .45's from the sheriff's desk and they went out after extinguishing the light. Crossing to the hotel, Two-Way in the lead, they entered the dim-lit lobby. The clerk behind the desk was the same one who had sold them the stage tickets—but he was asleep in his swivel chair, feet on the counter.

Two-Way held a finger to his lips and tiptoed over to the register, saw the number of McCandless's room and headed up the stair, Cardowan behind him.

Halfway up a figure appeared at the head of the stairs, a woman, and started to descend. She passed them without speaking, but as soon as she was out of sight, Cardowan grabbed Two-Way's elbow with a grip of iron.

"That's Shayne's daughter!" Cardowan said huskily. "The mine manager. She knows my face. Hell, we can't do it!"

For a long moment, they stared at each other, Two-Way swearing bitterly under his breath. Then he said hoarsely, "She's got to be kept out of the way! Slug her, gag her, do anything until I get McCandless out of town!"

"What if she's told McCandless already?"

"Would he be asleep here if she had? Now, go on. I'll go up to his room and spill it. You see she's out of the way."

Cardowan descended the stairs softly, while Two-Way hurried on up. At the angle of the stairs, which was just above the lobby desk and hidden by a partition, Cardowan stopped and flattened out against the wall to listen. Kate was talking to the clerk, and her voice was pleading.

"But don't you see I *have* to see him! It's terribly important!"

"Miss, I tell you again he was shot today. He's lost blood, and he's weak. Ain't his life more important than your news? I got doctor's orders to let no one see him."

"What's his room number?"

"I can't tell you that, Miss."

There was a pause, then Kate said, "Look here. If you were to lose a big fortune, a vast fortune, and getting it back depended on the way you used every minute, every hour, wouldn't you want somebody to tell you?"

"I reckon I would."

Kate said passionately, "Well, that's what I'm trying to tell him! He's losing a fortune every minute! Can't you see?"

The clerk said nothing for a moment, then sighed. "All right. I'll go up and see if he's in any condition to listen to you. You wait here."

Cardowan turned back and took the stairs two steps at a time. He dodged down a corridor to his right and waited until he heard the old man's steps, waited till he saw him reach the landing and turn down another corridor.

Then he descended the stairs quietly, his hat pulled down low on his forehead. He felt his palms sweaty, his heart pounding.

Kate was standing, her back against the counter, watching the staircase.

When Cardowan came down she glanced idly at him, then away. And then her glance returned to him.

He swung toward her, palming his gun out at the same time, and stopped. The gun was pointing at her, cocked.

"I've never shot a woman yet," he said thickly, flatly, quietly, "but there's always a first time."

Kate, her mouth half-open, looked into his face and shivered. His long jawline gave him a wolfish appearance, and the thin tight and unsmiling lips warned her of an iron determination. But it was his eyes, so cold, so shallow, so unblinking, hard and unpitying as a dead man's that carried the final and irrevocable warning.

She said, "What is it you want?"

"Come over here," Cardowan said, backing away. She followed him across the lobby, until they were standing by a good-sized rug.

"Lie down on the edge of that rug," Cardowan ordered.

For a moment Kate hesitated, and then she obeyed.

"Put your arms down at your sides."

She did. She lay on her back, looking up at him. He knelt by her and put the muzzle of his Colt at her brow, and with the other hand whipped out a soiled bandana.

"Open your mouth or I'll let this off," he said very quietly, with no emphasis, so that its very lack of any passion made her know it for the truth.

She opened her mouth and immediately he stuffed the handkerchief in it. "Can you breathe?" he asked.

She nodded.

"Then don't be afraid. I won't hurt you if you don't

make a fuss."

He lifted the corner of the rug over her and then proceeded to roll her up in it. Some panic seized her, and she struggled now, but it was too late. The first fold pinioned her arms. Cardowan rolled her down the whole length of it, picked the bulky burden up, holstered his gun and walked to the door with it over his shoulder. Outside on the porch he looked around, saw no one, and descended the steps.

He knifed in the space between the hotel and the adjoining building and leaned the rug up against the wall.

"Can you hear me?" he asked. "If you can, move."

There was a movement inside the rug.

"Can you breathe? Move if you can."

Again there was the movement.

"Then stand still. I'll be back in five minutes."

He drew a deep breath, brushed the dust off his shirt and strolled back up the steps into the lobby.

The clerk was standing there at the foot of the stairs, and Cardowan nodded idly.

"Where is she?" the clerk asked.

"Who?"

"A girl. Did she go out?"

"I met a gal crossing the street just as I came in," Cardowan said.

The clerk swore under his breath, then looked keenly at Cardowan.

"Say," he said suddenly. "Ain't you the partner to that ranny that bought six seats on the night stage?"

Cardowan nodded.

"Well, you damned near lost your freight, mister," the clerk said and smiled.

"It's right here," the clerk said, indicating the desk with a jerk of his thumb. "They waited for you and waited for you, and when you never showed up, they dumped it off here. I was aiming to tell Patterson down at the feed stable in case you asked about it, but I never got around to it."

Cardowan exhaled a long, shuddering breath, and watched the clerk walk around to the desk.

"See? Right here," the clerk said, and pointed.

"Good," Cardowan said calmly now. "I sort of figured you'd keep it." He leaned on the counter and said, "Did you just come from upstairs?"

The clerk said he had.

"Don't happen to know whether McCandless is awake, do you?"

"You too," the clerk replied, shaking his head. "Hell, yes, he's awake."

"Will he see me?" Cardowan asked huskily.

"I reckon not. That's what that girl wanted. He's talking to someone in his room, and he hollered through the door for me to go away."

That was all Cardowan wanted to know—that the clerk had not seen Two-Way. He straightened up, his fingers trembling. He said, "It don't matter. It can wait. Thanks."

He started for the door, then turned and said, "I'll go get a buckboard for that stuff. My partner and me are leaving town pretty quick."

The clerk nodded.

Cardowan turned again and started for the door, then paused and came back to the desk. He was smiling now. "Say," he began quietly. "Do you like a joke?"

"Sure," the clerk said.

"Well, I'm going to pull one on my partner. The damn fool got to winning in a card game tonight at the Maricopa and he wouldn't leave come stage time. He claimed you'd hold that freight over and then he forgot it. If you see him again don't say anything about it being here. I'll tell him it went out on the stage and that he's lost a prospecting outfit for good and all. How about it?"

The clerk chuckled. "Sure. I'll keep my mouth shut."

Cardowan nodded and grinned. "Teach that damn fool to gamble five hours at a stretch. Don't give me away now."

The clerk said he wouldn't. Cardowan bought him a cigar, waved a careless hand and left.

Upstairs, Two-Way was sitting in the seat by the table. McCandless, his face purple with anger, stood beside the bed, a gun in his hand, glaring at Two-Way.

"And you knew it all the time I was in that cell and you didn't tell me?"

"Don't be a damn fool, McCandless," Two-Way said dryly. "How could I? St. Vrain had a gun. I'm afraid of him. You are too. What could you have done?"

"And that other man there was Cardowan, the man who robbed the mine with St. Vrain?"

"Yes. That's the man. He's downstairs now, thinking I won't tell you his name." Two-Way smiled at the thought of the beauty of this doublecross, but he went on, "St. Vrain locked him in there along with me when he discovered I finally found out what he'd hired me for."

"Hired you for?"

"Yes. I was riding to Christian City. I met St. Vrain and Cardowan on the road at night just above the concessionaire's houses at the edge of the reservation. I knew St. Vrain, but not Cardowan. St. Vrain asked me if I wanted to earn a nice piece of money. I said sure. Then he told me to ride in with Cardowan to Fort Benjamin with these two pack horses, because they held something valuable and a gang of men were chasing him. These were Cardowan's own men, mind you. St. Vrain couldn't go because the army wanted him."

"But why didn't he send Cardowan in alone?"

Two-Way shrugged. "He's dumb. St. Vrain knew that. I reckon he figured he'd take a chance on the first man he could pick up rather than trust the bluff to Cardowan. He's like that, isn't he? Besides, there'd be a man along in case Cardowan tried to doublecross him."

McCandless nodded. "So you went in and claimed protection?"

"You heard St. Vrain say so."

"Then what?"

"The army gave us a guard almost to Rincon. St. Vrain beat us here and waited for us."

"But not before you hid the gold?"

"Yes. We hid it. A pack broke and a couple of the sacks rolled out and I discovered what it was. Cardowan covered me with a gun, then decided it was best to hide it while he took me to St. Vrain. When we met St. Vrain, he knew we couldn't buck his guns. He locked us up in jail here, and then tried to find out where we'd hid the gold."

McCandless was watching him closely, suspiciously, aware of the conviction in Two-Way's talk, and fighting it. "Then what was all this hocus-pocus about the papers you didn't want him to give me?"

Two-Way sighed, as if his patience was being tried, "But dammit, McCandless, don't you see? Those were the credentials of the other insurance man St. Vrain killed—Jake Finger. With you as a witness, he claimed he took those from me. If I didn't tell him where the gold was hid, he'd tell you of the theft and blame it on to me and Cardowan. There was all the evidence. All you'd have to do would be to ask the army. You'd have cut down on me with all that evidence, and I was innocent all the time." He raised his hands, palm out. "What would you have done? It meant my neck. I told him."

"He's after it now?"

"Sure. After he left we slugged the guard, got out of jail, and then Cardowan wanted me to bargain with you. We'd show you the gold if you'd give us a cut."

"But St. Vrain might have the gold now."

"Five hundred pounds," Two-Way said dryly. "How far could he get with that load? Besides, you won't be twenty minutes behind him if you move fast."

McCandless said slowly, "And why are you telling me this?"

Two-Way grinned. "I'm a gambler. I thought it might be worth a third of the gold to you. Is it?"

"What about Cardowan?"

"Take him. He's a killer and crook, and a fool."

"You don't mind a little doublecrossing, do you, my friend?"

"Not a bit," Two-Way said frankly. "I live by my wits."

McCandless looked at him with contempt. "A third of the gold. Eighty thousand dollars."

"That's it," Two-Way said quietly. "You write out a

check to me for eighty thousand dollars. I can lead you to St. Vrain and the gold. You'll have it by morning if you hurry. If you haven't got it by then, all you've got to do is send a man back to the bank and stop payment on the check. If you have, then I'll cash it and ride off."

McCandless looked at him for a long time, trying to find something to say, something to protect the hardness of this bargain. But he couldn't. Two-Way had beat him at his own game. He said, "I don't believe the gold's been stolen."

Two-Way reached in his pocket and pulled out the credentials of Herb Skelton, which Cardowan had given him. "There's the insurance papers I took from Cardowan when he was sleeping."

McCandless glanced at them and pursed his lips.

"Would you believe it," Two-Way said gently, making a wild, wild guess, "if I was to show you that Miss Kate Shayne, your mine manager's daughter, is registered here at this hotel looking for you to tell you about the steal?"

"I would," McCandless answered bluntly.

"Then come along."

Downstairs, before the silent clerk, Two-Way whirled the register around and pointed out Kate Shayne's name. McCandless stared at it.

"Is there a pretty, slight girl, blond, big blue eyes, registered here under the name of Kate Shayne?" McCandless asked the clerk.

"Sure. She's been looking for you. I told her—"

"Man!" Two-Way said angrily. "Are you going to stand there while he gets farther and farther away with the stuff? Come on!"

McCandless whirled and ran for the door. In five minutes men were streaming out of both saloons for the livery stable, Two-Way and McCandless in the lead. In another short five minutes there was a sizeable posse organized, and no one knew what for. McCandless had kept that to himself. Two-Way, in all that bustle, cast about for Cardowan, but he could not find him. Anyway, the fool had got the girl out of the way.

They rode out of town south in a thunder of hooves, and a thick cloud of dust slowly settling in the night silence behind them.

Cardowan stepped out of the passageway between the hotel and its adjoining building and hurried down to the feed stable.

He asked the night man to look at the horses for sale. By lantern light he picked out a pair of chunky bays.

"Are they stayers?" he asked.

"You wouldn't be paying what you are for them if they wasn't," the night man said. "I'm asking money for them."

"I'll take them. I want a buckboard too."

He bought a complete outfit, horses, harness and buckboard, and drove them off up the street. He went the full block and came around in the alley behind the hotel. Then he went in the back way and spoke to the clerk, whom he had to waken.

"Give me a lift with these, will you, Dad?"

"Sure." The clerk helped him carry out the two heavy bundles which he loaded on the buckboard.

"Your partner left, didn't he? With McCandless."

"Yeah. I'm following along now. I'll pick him up. What's the posse after?"

"Dunno. Mac wouldn't say."

"Leave it to my partner to get in one of them. Gambling and posses is his meat," Cardowan said, chuckling. "You never told him about this freight?"

The clerk said no, bade him good night, and Cardowan waved from the buckboard seat. As soon as the clerk went in, Cardowan dismounted and went over to the passage way between the two buildings. In a moment he returned with Kate Shayne wrapped in the rug. He hated to have to carry her along, but it would be suicide to leave her.

As it was he had a night's headstart on the crowd that would be sure to follow. There was a railroad back over the mountains and south, and once he reached there he would have safe transportation, the money and a clear road ahead.

Chucking the bundle in the buckboard he drove north

out of town, the way he had come in.

Once clear of the lights of town he took Kate down and unwrapped her.

For a long moment she sat on the seat and could not speak, her tongue numbed from the gag. When she found her voice, she asked huskily, "Where are you taking me?"

"Mexico, if you're good," Cardowan drawled. He looked obliquely at her and laughed softly. "It'll be a long pull, sister, but once I make it, I'll be in gravy."

She said nothing and he was silent for a moment. Then he looked suddenly at her. "*We'll* make it," he amended thoughtfully. "Why not?"

And as if he thought of something, he took the gun from his right holster and rammed it in his waistband at his left side.

Then he laughed—and she understood.

CHAPTER SIXTEEN

Poco KNEW THE ROUTE of the stage well, calculated its speed and his own and guessed he could overtake it around the ford of Roan River. He did not hurry. Two-Way and Cardowan would probably stay locked up for an hour or so, after which they would think a long while before they followed him. Providing they could round up a bunch of hard-cases in both saloons, they were sure to follow—but that would take time. And he would need a horse with a lot of bottom if he was to get this gold back across the mountains to Kate Shayne again.

Rocking along in the saddle, he thought of her now, and of the way he had seen her sleeping the morning he left her in the San Jons. What had she done when she reached the TC3 home spread and found McCandless gone? Possibly she had set out to find him, keeping the facts of the gold steal a secret, since she too knew the danger in spreading that news around. She would never rely on him to bring it back because she neither thought him able to do it, nor honest enough to. She had classed him with Cardowan, a killer and thief.

Well, he would show her that it didn't take a man to be honest and dull. He'd bring back her gold, laugh at her thanks and ride off.

Rousing from his reverie, he was aware that he had crossed the ford and by the light of the full moon he could see that the stage had turned off the road. The deep tracks of its wheel rims were gone.

He pulled up, puzzled, and turned back. On the other side of the ford he could see where the stage turned off on a side road, and immediately he understood. This was the trail to the TC3 spread, one of the McCandless holdings. Doubtless the stage had turned up this road to leave word of Abe McCandless's shooting, after which they would take the shortcut over the hills and pick up the stage road farther on.

He spurred ahead now on the main road and in another half hour came to the spot where the shortcut ran into the main road. There were no tracks on the shortcut, which meant he was in time.

He pulled his horse off the road, ground-haltered it in some screening mesquite, and then squatted in the shadow of piñon, turning over in his mind the best way of holding up the stage. Without rocks to roll in the road, or trees to drag across it, the stage would not stop at his command. And the guard could easily fight off a lone rider.

He stood up now and walked over to the end of the short-cut. Here the stage must climb a steep grade before it achieved the road again. He ran down the shortcut a few yards, then crouched in the shadow of a sprawling piñon. He heard the stage brakes scream as it hit the bottom of the grade, and then the sound of the slow and laboring horses swelled as the stage approached.

When it passed him he heard the deep breathing, the stomping, rhythmical clopping of the horses struggling for a sure foothold on the pebbly grade. There was a jingle of harness, a low conversation between two men, a curt, "Huddup, there," and the stage was by.

He left the piñon, ran lightly the few steps to the stage

and jumped for the iron rim on the rear guard's seat.
Catching it, he hung there a moment until the stage had
swung onto the road and the horses were whipped up into
a noisy trot, and then he swung himself up.

The guard and the driver were swaying to the jolting of
the stage, not talking, when Poco, gun in hand, erect on
top of the stage, drawled clearly from behind them,
"Howdy, gents."

It was the guard that whipped around and froze.

"Tell him to pull up," Poco said.

The driver slammed on the brakes and reined the two
teams up and the stage slammed to a screeching stop. Then
he turned and surveyed Poco. "Hello, Poco," he drawled.

"Howdy, Harry."

"Stick-up?"

"No. I just wanted to be sure you weren't nervous."

Harry laughed and spat loudly, imperturbably, as Poco
holstered his gun.

"What you got this trip, Harry?" Poco asked.

"Dunno. Junk, I reckon. We're traveling mighty light
and no passengers. Wanta look at the waybill?" And then,
before Poco could answer, Harry spat again and growled,
"What the hell are you—a growed man—doin' playin'
around with this business? Thought you never touched it."

"I don't."

"If you're startin', then I'm quittin', and that's a leddy-
mortal cinch."

Poco grinned. "I'm not. There was some freight put on
by mistake tonight. I knew you'd cut down on me if I tried
to stop you—cut down or run."

"Freight?" Harry asked slowly.

"Two pieces. Mighty heavy. Wrapped in tarps. A couple
of men bought places for it."

"Oh, that," Harry said, chuckling. "Well, Poco, you've
had a ride for nothin'. When those two passengers never
showed up we dumped the freight off at the hotel."

"Hotel?" Poco echoed. "In Rincon?"

"Sure. Go see Rus back there. He's got it stowed away
under the counter." When Poco groaned softly, Harry

said, "Hell, son, nobody'll take it if it's yours."

But Poco said nothing. He was thinking how inevitable it was that Two-Way or Cardowan or McCandless would stumble onto the gold and if it was McCandless who found it, his promise to Kate Shayne was for nothing. He'd be hunted the country over. Shayne would suffer at Abe's hands for the theft just the same. If Two-Way or Cardowan or both got it, then he still had a chance.

He squatted on his heels and built a smoke.

"Stop at the TC3?" he asked Harry.

"Yeah. The boys asked us to leave word there about Abe," Harry said, and added dryly, "That was some fancy shootin', Poco."

"I got a package to deliver to him, after I deliver it to somebody else first. And when I deliver it, I reckon I'll square things," Poco said.

Harry spat again. "It's goin' to make a lot of people happy when you do, Poco. Me included. You're the only man I ever knew that could work up the guts to try. Maybe when his mark is rubbed out, some of them ten counties of his will go back to the people he stole 'em from."

"What's that?" the guard asked, listening.

They fell silent. Riding down on the wind, there came the sound of many horses galloping.

Poco said quietly, "A posse after me, likely—or after what I'm after."

"They aim to take you?" Harry asked quickly.

"Likely."

Harry lifted the ribbons and said grimly, "Hold on, Poco. We'll see about that."

Poco put out his hand swiftly. "Huh-uh, Harry. Thanks. You'd never make it. My horse is back there a stretch and I couldn't reach him either, so I'll stick."

He rose and walked back to the rear seat. Harry clamped the brake again and the guard went up beside Poco. Soon, in the moonlight, they could see a body of horsemen emerge out of the night. In another minute twenty or thirty horsemen were pulling up in a moil of dust beside the stage.

"There he is," Two-Way called to a man across the road from him. This man, Poco could see, was McCandless, hatless, his arm in a sling, his shaggy head turned up.

"That's right," Poco drawled. "So what?" His Colts were resting easily in his palms, cocked, ready, hanging loose at his sides.

"Where is it?" McCandless asked curtly.

"Where is what?"

"You know damned well what we're talking about," Two-Way said.

Poco turned his head to look at Two-Way. "Careful, rat," he said quietly, and Two-Way kept quiet.

Then Poco turned to McCandless. "I took a run out to catch the stage south. Anything wrong with that?"

McCandless said nothing. He dismounted and walked up beside Harry.

"Any heavy freight this trip, Harry?"

"Nope," Harry answered indifferently.

"I'll look."

"Go ahead. Watch out for that wheel hoss. He's a shoe-pitcher."

No one talked while McCandless swung up on the hub of the front wheel and looked in the express compartment under Harry's feet. It was filled with old clothes, a rifle, a couple of light packages containing a lunch and a half-dozen boxes of shotgun shells. McCandless swung down and went to the rear of the stage, swung up on the hub, and looked at the rear boot. It was empty.

He climbed down and opened the door, struck a match and looked inside. Two dozen paper-and-canvas-wrapped parcels, all small, lay on the seat. He shook the biggest and found it light.

Then he turned and looked at Two-Way.

"On top," Two-Way said.

McCandless swung up to the top of the stage, walked its length and stopped beside Poco. He looked down at Two-Way now.

"Harry," he said, still looking at Two-Way, "I know you for a truthful man. Has Poco St. Vrain taken any freight—tarp-wrapped freight—off this stage tonight?"

"No," Harry said immediately, curtly.

"He lies!" Two-Way said angrily.

Harry laughed. Then no one spoke.

McCandless finally broke the silence by saying to Two-Way, "I see. You tolled me out of town while that partner of yours made off with it."

"I swear—" Two-Way began, and then he stopped.

McCandless's big thick fist had streaked down to his gun-butt—which wasn't there. Two-Way clawed frantically at his waistband. McCandless's single gun was slung from the hip below his sling-held arm, and only too late did he realize it. He crossed his hand across his belly and got the gun and drew it out backward, just as Two-Way's gun splintered the night with its roar. McCandless grunted, took a step backward to brace himself, at the same time fumbling with the gun to turn it around. He did, just as Two-Way shot the second time. McCandless's legs buckled and he went down on his knee, but his gun swung up in a racketing roar. Then Two-Way's joined in furious counterpoint.

And Poco, in that bedlam, his guns held loosely at his sides, standing immobile not three feet from McCandless, saw Two-Way jackknife over his saddle horn, shoot once into the road, then slide out of his seat.

Poco's gaze swiveled to McCandless. His head hung low on his chest, and he coughed once. And then before Poco could move, he slanted sideways over the edge of the stage and fell to the road. There was a dull, muscle-muffled snap as his back broke.

Three men dismounted and raced toward him.

Poco, looking down, said nothing until one man stood up and reported, "He was dead before he hit the road."

"What about Two-Way?" Poco asked.

"Dead," a voice announced.

"Which is damn well what you'll be, St. Vrain!" a voice called from the group of horsemen below. Poco shuttled his gaze to the horsemen, and saw the blunt nose of a shot-gun leveled at him.

"I dunno what this is all about," the voice continued, "but I heard that tinhorn say something to Mac about gold. Where is it, St. Vrain?"

"Yeah," another voice put in. "Have you got it, St. Vrain?"

There was a murmur among the men, and Poco recognized that growing madness which drives a mob to do insane things. Singly these men would not have spoken, but they were a mob now, and their leader, the man who cowed them, was dead.

"Who are you, there with the greener?" Poco drawled.

For answer, there was a husky laugh, and immediately Poco recognized it as the man who had called him a bogus badman that afternoon.

"You'll never know, hard-case," the man said.

"Put that gun down, Hank!" a man ordered from deep in the crowd.

"Just a minute," Hank said. "I may have to blow it out of him."

"You won't shoot," Poco said calmly, wishing it were the truth. "You can't."

"Why not?" Hank asked.

Poco considered a moment. He knew the men in this posse were divided, but it was the men in front, men like Hank, who could do the harm before the others made reason rule. The only thing left, then, the only thing that would satisfy these men suddenly liberated from a tyrant, was the gold.

"Play it close, Poco," Harry said.

Poco said, "I know where the gold is. I'll make a deal with you. I take you to the gold and you let me ride off."

"How much gold?"

"Enough," Poco answered.

And now a rider pushed his way through the crowd up to Hank and knocked the shotgun down.

"All right, St. Vrain," this man said. "It's a bargain. Maybe we'll get some of that back pay now. Get down off that stage, and drop those guns before you come."

Harry, from the seat, said to Poco in a low voice, "Know

where it is, Poco?"

"I know where it was," Poco answered grimly. "It won't be there now."

"Want to try a getaway?"

"Huh-uh. Thanks, Harry."

Under the posse's guns, to the company of Harry's muttered profanity, Poco shinnied down the stage and was searched for hide-outs. A man went for his horse, while others tied McCandless's and Two-Way's limp bodies on their horses. Strangely, Poco felt no emotion at the thought of McCandless's death. It had to come sooner or later, and now it was done.

The stage was ordered on, and Poco watched it drive off.

"What happened to that fellow with the tinhorn?" Poco asked one of the possemen. "Didn't he come with you?"

"Wasn't nobody with the tinhorn except McCandless," was the reply.

Then Cardowan was almost certain to have it, Poco reflected. And before he could get Cardowan, he would have to shake this stubborn pack of buzzards, but how, he didn't know.

In a few more minutes they were ready to leave. Poco was tied on his horse, placed in the middle of the posse, and they started off to town. He let the whole course of this wild chase run through his head, marveling at what men would do for gold, himself included, and wondering if returning it to Kate Shayne was worth it.

The ride was dusty, and the posse was in ill-humor and sleepy. Around daylight, just as the street was graying out of its shadow, the cavalcade reached Rincon.

Hank said, "Where to?"

"The hotel," Poco said, and yawned.

They dismounted and stomped up the steps, Poco in the lead. He hoped the gold would not be there. The clerk roused sleepily from a cot in the back office and came out to the desk, his eyes widening at the sight of this crew of grim-faced men.

Poco said, "A couple of men ordered some freight sent out on the night stage south. The driver said it was dumped off here. Where is it?"

"Gone," the clerk said bluntly. "One of them partners, the long, drawling gent, took it."

"When?"

"Close to midnight."

Poco turned to confront the men and shrugged. "Any of you know who that 'long drawling gent' was?"

"Who?" Hank asked.

"Espey Cardowan," Poco said quietly. He turned to the staring clerk. "How'd he get it out?"

"I helped him load it on a buckboard. I never knew it was that killer."

Poco smiled crookedly and turned to Hank. "Cardowan runs with about twenty men," he drawled quietly. "They were likely waiting outside town. Any of you hardcases feel like riding them down and taking it away from them?"

Then Hank started to curse him with blustering mouth-filling oaths. Poco looked bored. He leaned against the counter, listening idly to the muttering of the posse, looking at the register. Suddenly he bent down to examine a name, then straightened up and said swiftly to the clerk, "Who is Kate Shayne? Pretty, light-haired, got eyes that are mighty blue?"

"That's her," the clerk said absently. "She was registered here, but she disappeared around midnight. She ain't in her room and I can't find her."

Poco swallowed and stared at him. Hank had quit cursing now, looking at him. "What time did you say Cardowan left?"

"Close to midnight."

Poco felt a cold flush of panic creeping through his veins. He said softly, "Midnight. Did Cardowan see her, this Kate Shayne?"

The clerk said, "He said so."

And then Poco turned away, sick. Cardowan had her, of course. He had to take her or else she would give him away, and the thought of that clean, beautiful girl in Cardowan's hands made Poco rage. He tried to fight out of his mind what would happen, but he could not. He would have to get out of here, and do it quick. He beat down his anger into some semblance of control, and drawled to Hank, "Trot along, Big Wind. The gold's gone for good."

Hank swung the shotgun up pointing at Poco's belly. "You know where Cardowan is, unless I'm wide of a damned good guess. You're goin' to take us to him. We'll take care of those twenty hard-cases of his—and yours too."

Poco said "No."

Hank nosed the shotgun higher. "If I was you, I'd hate to get a hole blowed through my belly just because I acted like a mule."

"No," Poco said quietly, menacingly. "I don't know where he is. I'm sleepy."

"You'll be—"

And then a voice from the stairs cut in and took up Hank's unfinished sentence with, "Tried by a jury and sentenced."

Poco turned and looked at the stairs. Sam Van, thumbs rammed in his belt, stood regarding the crowd, his face grim, his jaw outthrust a little.

He came down the few steps and walked over to Poco, saying to Hank, "Put up that greener."

Hank swiveled it to him now. "Who the hell are you, Mister?"

"I said 'Put it up.'"

"And I said stand still or I'll make you!"

Van and Hank glared at each other. Poco, looking at them, knew that Van's bluff wouldn't work.

"Now get the hell out of here while you still can!" Hank said curtly.

Van replied, "I'm going to reach in my shirt pocket for something, fella. If you're wise, you won't shoot till you see it."

He reached up slowly to his shirt pocket, drew forth a metal badge, and handed it to Hank.

Hank read loud, "United States Marshal."

Poco looked swiftly at Van, who was watching Hank.

Van reached out for his badge. "You'll turn that man over to me, boys, to be tried and convicted and sentenced according to law."

For a moment they were silent, then someone said, "What for?"

"For the theft of a quarter million dollars worth of gold."

"Whose gold?" Hank asked.

"McCandless's."

Then a man in the crowd growled, "To hell with you, Lawman! McCandless is dead. That gold belongs to whoever gets it, and St. Vrain can take us to it. He's our prisoner."

"To take our orders or hang, by God!" Hank added.

Van said, "Mob law, huh? All right, maybe this will stop you." He stepped forward, raised his voice so that everyone in the room could hear him. "I hereby declare every man in this crowd conscripted as an emergency deputy United States Marshal. You're all now drawing the wages of the United States Government, serving under the rules and regulations prescribed by law. You're all answerable to me for the safe conduct of the government's prisoner to the Marshal's Office in Phoenix. If this prisoner comes to any harm at your hands, the lot of you will be prosecuted by the government. And"—here he paused, to make sure of their attention—"the government can call out the army to hunt every one of you down or chase you out of the country."

It was their surprise, their momentary forgetting of him, that Poco had been waiting for. Every man in the crowd was watching Van, who was two steps to the side of Poco.

Poco slowly tensing his muscles, leaped to one side and in behind Van, wrapped an arm around Van's waist, and with the other whipped up one of Van's guns and covered the crowd from under Van's arm. It was so sudden coming on the heels of the announcement that it caught them all flat-footed, Hank included.

"Now, gents," Poco drawled. "Cut down on me and you kill a United States Marshal, your boss. Just to keep you from doin' it, I'll leave and take your boss with me."

He flipped out Van's other gun, rammed it in his back and said, "Sam Van, you back up to those stairs. And don't dodge."

Van had no choice. He started backing toward the stairs, shielding Poco from the guns of the mob.

Suddenly Hank yelled, "Prisoner's escapin'? If the boss gets killed while we're tryin' to take the prisoner, that's his hard luck!"

He started to raise the shotgun. Poco's gun roared once, and Hank took a long step backward, his gun clattering to the floor, a faint look of surprise washing over his face before his knees buckled and he pitched forward on his face. The clerk ducked behind the counter.

Poco whirled Van away from him, saying swiftly, "Get up those stairs, you fool! They won't take this!"

Van legged it up the stairs. Poco took the steps two at a time, then dodged to one side of the stairwell where Van was waiting.

Poco handed him a gun and said, "Nice bluff. Now let's go. It worked." Van took the gun without a word, then turned it on Poco, and rammed it in his midriff. "I meant it," he drawled slowly, quietly. "I'm a U.S. Marshal and you're under arrest. My prisoner. Give me that gun."

In the thick silence that followed, Poco looked closely at Van, heard the mob thundering up the steps and knew he was licked, and that Cardowan was gone with Kate. Van would have shot him down, and he knew it. He handed the gun over, saying, "That's tough. They'll get you along with me."

Van motioned him around a corner of the corridor, and said quietly, "Out that end window on to the awning-roof."

Poco ran the few steps to the window, opened it and climbed out.

"Now down the post to the street."

Poco shrugged, made his way down the corrugated tin of the roof to the corner, then swung himself down while Van watched from the room. A Negro, broom in hand, utterly still, watched them from across the street.

"Now run for the jail," he commanded, "and don't make a break for it, son. I can shoot."

Poco turned and streaked across the street for the sheriff's office. He achieved it without a shot being fired and rocketed through the door. Seizing a rifle from the wall rack, he leaped to the window, knocked out a pane, and poked the gun through. Van had already shinnied down the porch post, and was starting across the street. Two men boiled out of the hotel door, and stopped when they caught sight of him.

In that moment of watching, Poco had made up his mind to throw down on Van and drive him away from the jail, but when he saw one of the possemen raise his gun and start to lower it for a steady aim at Van's back, he switched his sight around and shot blindly.

He saw the man go down, saw his partner dodge into the hotel again, and heard him yell for help.

Van, on the near sidewalk now outside the sheriff's office was talking rapidly, and Poco heard him say to the sweeper, "You take this money, buy the fastest horse in town and ride for the army over at Fort Benjamin. If you kill your horse, buy another. Only *get the hell there in a hurry* and bring them back here. Got it?"

"Yassuh. I'se gone, boss," the Negro replied.

A second later three men ran out of the hotel door and flipped a shot at Van. The Negro had ducked out of sight down a side street. Van lunged through the doorway, slammed it shut and faced Poco's leveled rifle.

He smiled a little and said, "That won't get us anywhere, St. Vrain."

Poco said softly, his voice choked with anger, "I don't know why I didn't cut down on you out there in the street. You've—" his voice trailed off. What was the use telling him of Kate Shayne. He wouldn't believe it, and he couldn't do anything about it if he did.

"I know why you didn't," Van replied. "You aren't a killer, son. You may be a thief, but not a killer. I reckoned on that."

"I hope you're satisfied, you damn bounty-hunting hero!" Poco said.

"You didn't know it, son, but I was put here to watch out for that gold shipment. I got evidence from those two hard-cases that you were the one that stole it." A shot ripped through the window now, followed by another. "I'll take you in to face the music—if we can fight off this mob till the army gets here."

Poco's eyes blazed. He wanted to take the butt of his rifle and smash Van's face in, but suddenly he knew this was wrong, that Van had only done his duty as a lawman, his simple honest and capable best.

A slug ripped through the window and dust sifted down from the sidewall, and it was still. Poco rubbed a trembling hand over his face and took a deep breath and lowered his rifle.

"All right," he said tonelessly, and smiled crookedly. "It looks like we're in the soup together."

He didn't care much whether they got through it or not. Every hour they spent fighting off this mob, Cardowan would be taking Kate closer to Mexico. He couldn't leave her—unless he shot her. Poco, his face gray, turned to Sam Van. He wanted someone to talk to him, wanted to hear a voice, wanted to do anything but think.

"Here's your pile of cartridges," Van said calmly. "Make them count."

CHAPTER SEVENTEEN

H ARRY PARKHOLDER, squat, heavy, wide-shouldered, unshaven, in the tradition of stage drivers, freighters and muleskinners, was a hardbitten man and quite naturally fearless. He hated just two things above all else: beer, which was a bellywash for children, and injustice. He hated the latter more than the former.

When he whipped his team away from the posse that night, leaving Poco St. Vrain in hostile hands, he was mad clean through. However, he had the wisdom to see that while majorities are often wrong, when the majority is a mob it is always right—as far as going against it is concerned.

But he liked Poco St. Vrain. He remembered the time Poco loaded one of the stages he was driving on the Whitewater run with his own crowd and fought off a gang of cutthroat killers just for the fun of it. He remembered too that Poco St. Vrain had never held up a stage, that he respected the men who drove them who, God knows, had a hard enough time as it was without fighting off holdups. In half a lifetime of knocking around on top a rolling stage, feeling the tug of the ribbons and the kickback of the brake and the exhilaration of sawing six half-wild horses over a snaky mountain road, Harry had met all kinds of outlaws, over a whisky and over a gunbarrel, but he had never met one—or who was called one—like Poco.

And right now, he reflected, ignoring his companion, the guard, Poco was in trouble.

He didn't say a word to his companion for a half hour, and then, spitting placidly and expertly into the wind, he whipped the horses into a fast trot.

"What's the hurry?" the guard asked.

"Business," Harry answered.

When he saw the upstage heave into sight ahead in the moonlight, he whoaed the horses, set the brake, wrapped the lines around it and climbed down. Erect, he was squat, unshaven, ragged and solid looking. The upstage pulled to a howling stop and Harry walked forward to exchange amenities.

When they were over, Harry said, looking up at the driver, "Wanta finish my run for me, Lew?"

Lew swore good-naturedly and wound the ribbons around the brake. "I just took over, but I never turned down a chanst to sleep yet. Sure."

He swung down, and when he was on the ground, Harry

asked, "Any passengers?"

"Two to Rincon."

"Uh-huh." If Lew had been listening, he might have detected a note of satisfaction in that grunt. Harry gestured over his shoulder to the downstage. "Watch out for that wheeler, he's a salty son—" he paused. "Are there any women inside?"

"Both men."

Then Harry good-naturedly finished naming the wheel-horse, waved his guard good-by, and climbed up to the seat of the upstage.

In less than a minute he had it out of sight of the downstage, heading for Rincon at a speed that choked off any objections the passengers might make.

It was well after sunup when he pulled into Rincon, and when the rumble of the stage died down a bit, he could immediately pick up the sound of gunfire over the town. Swinging into the main street, he was flagged to a halt by one of the possemen holding a rifle.

"What's goin' on here?" Harry called down.

"You better take her in the alley behind the hotel. There's a couple of hombres forted up in the jail and the boys are tryin' to smoke 'em out."

Harry grinned, knowing that would be Poco, wheeled the stage around, sought the back alley and pulled up behind the hotel, where the two passengers climbed out and received their luggage.

Then he took the stage down to the stable, pulled up beside the feed lot and left orders with the stableman to take his time in changing teams, since he had a little business upstreet.

Harry was not a stranger in Rincon, but neither was he well known, so that his presence did not create much notice in the face of all the shooting that was going on. All the stores across from the jail had been commandeered, including the hotel, and a scorching crossfire had cleared the street. Out of gun-range, the store doors were jammed with people discussing the situation.

The Maricopa Saloon could be approached from the

direction of the feed stable, and Harry made for it.

Inside, the barkeep was serving a few of the possemen who had come around by a circuitous route. Only one table, still lighted by the overhead lamp, was seating a poker game. The dance floor was empty and the girls were in their cribs upstairs sleeping off the night hours.

At the bar Harry asked of the barman, "Which room's Steamboat got? I got word for her that come in on the upstage."

"Leave it."

"Huh-uh. Private."

The barkeep studied him in ill-natured silence, then said, "Last door on your right at the end of the hall."

Harry climbed the stairs to the balcony, off which ran a long corridor onto which many doors opened. He knocked at the last, and was immediately bid come in.

Steamboat was standing at the window, still wearing the purple silk dress which showed off her slim, full-busted figure to dangerous perfection. When she looked at Harry, her dark eyes were sultry with anger, and her pert, powered little face twisted grotesquely in a crooked little smile.

"Hello, Ape," she said dispiritedly, and turned to look out the window again.

Harry smiled a bit forlornly, closed the door behind him and looked at the small bed in the corner. It was unmussed. His gaze shuttled to her, and he shifted his chew so it would be out of the way of his speech.

"You're worryin' too, huh?"

"Why shouldn't I?" Steamboat said savagely. "They'll kill him, a better man than the lot of them together."

"What happened?"

"Nobody'll talk, but he's forted up with a U.S. Marshal that's arrested him. I don't know why. I think a gang of this saloon riffraff is after his bounty."

Harry whistled under his breath. "Just two of 'em? It won't be another hour before somebody thinks to burn 'em out."

"Yes," Steamboat said bitterly. She walked across the

room then returned to the window and looked out, her face dark and brooding and sullen.

"You sort of like him, don't you, kid?" Harry asked.

"I'd die for him if it would help," she said simply.

Harry said quietly, "He's too good to go that way."

She turned slowly and her dark eyes held his. "Yes. Are we going to let them do it?"

"That's what I came up for."

He walked over to the bed and sat down on its edge, folding his hands before him.

Steamboat said bitterly, "I've tried to get a bunch up to fight them off, but do you think I can? No. They're like dogs. They're afraid of him when he's loose. It's 'Yes, Poco, why sure, Poco, just as you say, Poco, please, Poco, you're right, Poco,' but when he's down, they jump on the pile like alley curs!" She shrugged. "What can we do alone?"

Harry thought a minute. "You know, he must have a hard-shootin' rifle over there. I notice nobody is on the store roofs because those slugs likely tear through the false fronts."

Steamboat said nothing.

"What I was getting at," Harry said patiently, "is this. If they ain't on the roofs, they can't see us if we're on 'em. That there sheriff's office is bound to have a stove, and a stove has to have a pipe that sticks through the roof."

"Well?"

"I can buy a saw here and you can slip it down to them through the pipe hole. If I did it, this here marshal might suspect I was tryin' to help Poco escape. They saw through the roof and then we can load them on the upstage, knock the marshal in the head, cut loose one horse and Poco's made his getaway."

Steamboat considered a few seconds, and then she truly smiled, a smile of hope.

"Remember," Harry pointed out, "if this jasper is a U.S. Marshal, we'll have to dodge till this blows over. If they get you, it's just plain tough."

Steamboat said slowly, huskily, "I don't mind that.

Poco St. Vrain has got me out of a dozen jams, loaned me money, nursed me when I was sick over in Silver City, fought for me and crippled men that didn't treat me right. I never claimed to deserve it, Harry, but he's treated me white all down the line. I'd do anything, *anything* to pay back some of it."

Harry nodded and stood up. "I'll go buy a saw. You write a note to the marshal."

After some careful maneuvering outside to avoid the blistering fire that was lacing the street, Harry ended up in a hardware store where he bought a brace and bit, a saw and a length of rope.

Steamboat was waiting in her room when he returned. She had not even taken time out to change her clothes.

She led Harry across the hall to a vacant room that looked out on the roofs of the adjoining buildings to the flat, tar-paper-covered roof of the jail.

Harry opened the window and let her down the eight feet to the neighboring roof, then followed her. Their course was easy, demanding only that they make the crossing from one ridged roof to another with care. The solid row of false fronts on the street shielded them from view. Once the jail roof was reached, they had to crawl on their stomachs to the farthest of two stove pipes which jutted up through the roof.

Reaching it Harry pulled off the pipe, then took the bundle of tools and the note and motioned for Steamboat to take over.

He whispered. "You *got* to make him believe it, kid. You *got* to."

CHAPTER EIGHTEEN

WHEN THE PIPE was twisted off a shower of soot sanded down to the floor. Poco, kneeling under the window, was the first to see it. He signaled Van at the other window, who turned. Poco's six-gun was out, ready, for he expected to see an arm, gun in hand, appear through the hole.

Instead, a strange bundle of tools, a paper wedged in the handle of a saw, was lowered by a rope. Poco was closest and he crawled to it keeping low so that the slugs which were raining in through the window could not reach him. Van made no attempt to answer the fusillade, since their ammunition was low and a good bit of it had been used up in driving off the first rush before the besiegers settled down to blast them out.

The note was addressed: "U.S. Marshal."

Poco pulled the rope through and crawled over to Van and handed him the note, then took a rifle and began a sparse fire.

Van read the note and motioned Poco down.

"A trick," Van said. "Read it."

Poco read it quickly and looked up.

"That's no trick. I know her."

"It could still be a trick," Van said slowly.

Poco shrugged and indicated the ammunition. "I'm the prisoner, Lawman. But if you ever want me to stand trial, or live to see me, then you better take it. We can't hold out long at this rate."

"She says they'll fire the place soon. There's talk of it. And once we're driven into the jail we'll never saw through that roof. It's double tinned."

Van pursed his lips thoughtfully, while Poco built a cigarette with assumed indifference and watched him covertly.

"Maybe you're not a marshal after all," Poco drawled suddenly. "Are you afraid to commandeer that stage? Or are you waiting for the army to help you take me?"

Van only stared at him and said nothing. Then he looked at the frugal heap of ammunition, which, along with what was in their belts, would have to last them till help came.

He said, "You know her, you say? A honky-tonk chippie."

"Easy," Poco said warningly. "I'm an outlaw too. She's a good girl, a friend to me. That stage-driver is a friend of hers, or she couldn't offer us this. Watch your tongue.

"So much of a friend she'd turn a bunch of gunnies loose on me."

"Listen," Poco said slowly. "If you like someone, would you rather see them tried and jailed or cut down by a mob?"

Van said. "Put a couple of shots out there."

Poco rose and looked out. He saw a hat peep out from a store door, leveled his rifle, tied in his sights, pulled the trigger, and watched the hat fly back into darkness. A scorching blast of slugs rained into the wall in answer.

He squatted again and looked at Van.

"They'd find out," Van said. "When we don't shoot, they'll take a *pasear* over here and see why."

"Not for an hour or so. In their place would you risk it?"

"But they'll find out."

"And how will they know where we've gone?"

Van raised his gaze to Poco. "And you'll make a break for it the first chance you get?"

"Of course. But I'm not a killer."

"It don't matter to me if you are. I want to take you."

Poco shrugged indifferently. "All right, we stick."

"No, we won't," Van said suddenly. "We'll go. I think I'm a better man than you are, son. I'll show you."

Van moved over to the far window and threw a slow fire into one of the far stores. The fire which he drew in return came at such an angle that the stove in the corner was untouched.

Meanwhile, Poco, standing on the table, used the brace and bit to bore four holes at the points of a square, which he joined with a sawed line. Twenty minutes work and a square of the roof dropped down into his hands. It left an opening large enough to climb through.

Van had been easing off his fire now, so that the cessation of their gunfire would not seem too sudden.

Now he leveled his rifle at Poco and said, "Shed the guns, son. If we're crowded you'll get 'em back."

Poco obeyed.

"Now climb down off that table and squat in the

corner here. I'll go first."

Again Poco obeyed and Van placed a chair on the table. Then, gun in hand, so that he took no chances, he climbed up on the chair, straightened up suddenly and appeared to Steamboat on the roof with a gun in hand, pointed toward her.

She said gravely. "All right. I'm unarmed, you can see. Come on."

Van climbed out.

"Lie down," she whispered.

Then Poco appeared in the opening and hoisted himself through. He lay down by Steamboat and said. "Good girl, Steamboat. Thanks."

Van watched them a second, then he said to Steamboat. "You really like him?"

She only nodded.

"Enough to get down there and keep shooting as long as your ammunition holds out?"

Again she nodded, when Poco put in, "Huh-uh. No go, Lawman."

Van said stubbornly, "I'm running this. If she wants you alive, let her do it. You won't stop her. If she wants you dead, then she can leave. I'm obliged to her, but it's only half a job she offered."

"I was going down when you left," Steamboat said coldly. "I don't need a tin star and a gun to rawhide me into this, Mister." Van flushed. Poco said quietly, "You send her down there, Van, and I'll stand up and give myself up. Take your choice."

Van inched his Colt over till it covered Poco. "You try it and you'll live five seconds less than you would if you reached the roof-edge."

"Go on," Steamboat said. "I can take care of myself, Poco. Go on."

She said that Harry would pull the stage up beside the end building of the block just as soon as he, standing in the stable door, saw their signal from the roof. The road went right out past it. He would pull up, plead that he had forgotten his gloves which he would leave back in the stable, and during the time he was gone Van and Poco could drop down on the stage.

Then she turned to Poco and smiled crookedly. "You're a right hombre, Poco. I'm paying back my debts."

She leaned over and kissed him on the mouth, then before he could stop her, she crawled down through the hole. He made one desperate effort to grab her, but Van said quickly, "Easy."

Cursing, he saw her disappear below and in another few seconds the shooting started again from the sheriff's office below.

Van said, "Go ahead of me."

They reached the hotel, climbed through the window, crossed the corridor to Steamboat's room, and dropped down to the neighboring roof from her window. The rest of the way over the roofs of a dozen one-story buildings was easy. Van ordered Poco to go ahead, and he kept a gun in his hand the whole way.

On the roof of the end building, Van crawled along the ridgepeak to the false-front, took off his hat and looked over.

There, below and across the way, lounging in the wide door of the stable, was Harry, smoking a cigarette and talking with the stable attendant.

He looked up casually, saw Van, talked a few more seconds, then flipped his cigarette away and, along with the attendant, turned and vanished inside.

In another minute, the empty stage thundered through the door arch and swung out into the street and crossed it, pulling even with the end building, a saddle shop. Suddenly the brakes screamed on and Harry pulled the stage in close to the building.

When Van saw him go back to the feed stable, he waited only long enough to make sure the attendant went back with him, then he turned to Poco.

For a moment he debated whether to go down first or to order Poco to, but when he looked at Poco sitting atop the ridge boards and smoking indifferently, he made up his mind. He had known Poco just long enough to understand that when he looked the sleepiest, he was the most dangerous. Chances were, if he was to go down first, Poco would streak down the other side, drop to the ground, steal a horse and ride free.

Van smiled at his own wisdom. "You first," he said, pointing with the gun. "And stay away from those horses."

Cigarette in the corner of his mouth, Poco crept down to the eave, looked around, saw no one, then dropped to the top of the stage. He looked up.

"Get inside," Van ordered from the eave.

Poco dropped to the ground between the stage and the building, opened the door and climbed in. There on the back seat lay a single-action Colt .45, just waiting to be picked up. Poco scooped it up with one hand, sat down in the corner and wedged the gun under him. He knew now who it was driving the stage, and smiled a little. He was still smiling when Van swung in and sat in the opposite corner and hunkered down, motioning Poco to do the same. Then they waited for interminable minutes until they heard a man trotting toward them.

Harry did not even look inside as he swung up on the wheel hub, waved to a stable attendant, climbed up on the seat and whipped the horses into motion. Smoothly, the stage rolled out of town and the horses settled down to the light pull.

Harry did not drive fast because it would have attracted notice. Poco, sitting relaxed in the seat, was thinking of him, and of Steamboat, too. The thought of her back there alone, fighting off that saloon riffraff so he could escape, was intolerable. But the thought of Kate Shayne traveling with that killer of Cardowan was more intolerable. He closed his eyes, his thoughts a somber and sorrowful music in his brain. If he went back to Rincon and drew the mob away from Steamboat, it meant that finding Kate Shayne and Cardowan would be postponed, perhaps forever. He would have to first shake the posse, wasting precious hours of travel. For he knew with absolute certainty that Cardowan was heading for the railroad, because there was no other way he could elude inevitable pursuit and still keep the gold. Six hours head-start, with a bare fifty miles to the railroad, would work out nicely for him. And once aboard the train he was gone for good. Steamboat, trouper that she was, would have to drink the brew she had cooked up for herself and that Van had forced down her throat.

He was brought out of his reverie by the slowing of the stage. Van was leaning forward in his seat, gun in hand, and when the stage stopped, he leaped out and swiveled the gun up to cover Harry.

"Shuck 'em out, Mister," he said good-naturedly. "You've got me out of a jam, but I can't take a chance that you'll put me in another."

Poco heard the chuckle and knew it was Harry's.

"Sure," Harry said obligingly. "There's a rifle in the cupboard here if you can reach it."

Van swung up on the wheel-hub. Noiselessly, Poco stepped out of the stage, his gun poised, and waited. Harry saw and winked broadly, and Poco winked back. When Van had secured the rifle from the express compartment, he stepped down—into Poco's gun jamming him in the back.

"Steady," Poco said softly. "I won't shoot. Only drop there."

Van stood motionless holding his breath.

Harry drawled dryly, "Even a U.S. Marshal knows what to do when a gun's in his back, don't he?"

"Yes," Van said. He dropped the Colt and the rifle and turned to confront Poco. Poco did not smile, for he knew what Van was thinking, and felt a pity for him.

Van looked up at Harry now. "You can't get away with it. You'll have to answer some time."

"I figgered on that," Harry replied evenly. "I got to answer for a lot of things, some I like to, and some I don't. I like to answer for the favors Poco's done me, Lawman. I kin take care of the others." Then he said to Poco, "What'll it be, Poco? Go ahead or take a horse?"

Poco did not answer just then. He prodded Van up ahead of the horses, then examined the road, looking for some signs to back up the clerk's evidence. Guessing that Cardowan would hit for the nearest railroad point, which was over the San Jons, it followed that he would choose the quickest way over the trail. And there, fresher than any tracks except those of the single horse of the Negro who was on his way to Fort Benjamin, were the tracks of a team pulling a buckboard.

Van, watching him, guessing what he was doing, said, "You aren't going to follow him?"

"'Them,' you mean," Poco said somberly. "Kate Shayne is with him. I'm going to get him and the gold."

Van said slowly, "You mean, you're going to stick to it, when you'll have me, a posse of hard-cases and the U.S. Army on your tail by night?"

"That's right," Poco answered.

To Harry, he said, "Anything against driving the legs off these horses, Harry, if I make it good, along with two fares?"

"That ain't—"

"I'm paying," Poco cut in. "You'll be in enough of a jam without catching hell from your boss. Will you fog it?"

"You watch," Harry said, nodding.

Once the rifle and Van's gun were deposited under Harry's feet, Poco motioned Van into the stage and they were off again. Poco leaned against the side wall, his feet on the seat, the gun in his lap. He made no move to force Van to get out and thereby lighten the stage, and Van did not offer to do so. Without him saying it, Poco guessed that Van would have refused, would have to be clubbed into it. There was a hard grain of stubbornness about this marshal that Poco recognized and liked, perhaps because there was the same grain in him.

CHAPTER NINETEEN

KATE SHAYNE WAS AFRAID to go to sleep, even if she had been able to. Even watching Cardowan in that thin moonlight, she was afraid, and she crowded against the end of the buckboard seat, stiff with panic. A little thread of remembered conversation kept running through her mind, things Poco St. Vrain had said of the outlaw Espey Cardowan that night at supper up on the peak. She had forgotten it, but now all those hints as to his cruelty, his savage delight in working his bloody will, came unbidden to her mind.

Too, she recalled all those things she had spoken to Poco up there on the peak that night, hard and chiding things that blamed him for his way of life and his arrogance and his toughness. But now she would have given anything for some of his hardness, his cunning with guns, his mocking courage. Somehow, the memory of those chill dark eyes was comforting. Hadn't he said he would get the gold back? Didn't they have the gold here? Wouldn't he follow and overtake them? And when he does, she thought with shame, I will be proud of the murder in his eyes, that hard, unbending arrogance of his that will let him kill.

But in those hours before he came she must face this out. And since she was a reasonable girl, she decided the best way to act would be to keep quiet. She did. Up the long grade of the San Jons, Cardowan rolled many cigarettes and smoked them down without looking at her. His attention was on the horses, and he kept them working with that same ruthless threat that he used to drive men.

On the downgrade it was a different story. Even the light of the moon could not keep it from turning into a nightmare. For the grade was steep, the buckboard had no brakes, and it was carrying a full eight hundred pounds. It meant one thing, that the horses would have to keep out of the way of its ponderous weight, and the only way they could do this was to run. The road snaked and twisted around deep canyons, a sheer wall on one side, a sheer drop on the other, knifing its way around a dozen hairpin turns and switchbacks.

Only a man who knew and could dominate horses, a

man with an iron nerve, a love of danger, thought-quick judgment—or a dead drunk man—would have tried it. Cardowan was all of these—sure, quick, reckless, and drunk with the knowledge that victory was only a matter of a few more hours.

He had the good sense to give his horses their heads, checking them firmly, whipping them only as punishment and not to gain speed. He sawed them close at the curves, skidding the buckboard in long, reckoned curves that more than once set the off-wheels over the edge, only to whip up the team into taking the weight in time to yank it back. They lunged down gulleys, forded streams in a thundering shimmer of rainbows in the moonlight and took the straight stretches of dark pine-shadowed road with insane swiftness.

When Kate reached that bottom of fear when panic ceases and excitement is almost a lust in the blood, she liked it. She knew she was riding with a man whose cold, sure judgment of horses was instinctive and unerring. Dawn caught them nearly in the foothills, where the grade had lengthened out. The horses were almost foundered and welcomed the slow pace Cardowan chose now.

While still in the foothills, Cardowan took a side road that turned south along the base of the San Jons. It was only a rough wagon road. After traveling it for an hour, they pulled into a clearing which held a log shack, a slab shed and a pole corral in which a half-dozen horses were eyeing them.

Cardowan pulled up here, eyeing the man standing in the door of the shack, a roughly-dressed and suspicious homesteader by his looks.

He said softly to Kate, "I wouldn't try to drive off if I was you. There are fresh horses here, you see."

"Yes."

He looked at her and smiled wolfishly. "Your part's to keep your mouth shut—always. You better learn it."

He climbed down stiffly from the buckboard, waved to the man and started across to him.

Kate saw them conversing, then the man turned and

entered the shack, Cardowan following him. When he was gone, Kate looked around her. There was thick screening timber surrounding her, which, once she was in it, would hide her. Cardowan could not search for her long, since his every action had spoken of his haste. The edge of the timber dipped close to the house at one point, and that would be the place to enter it. She eyed it for a few desperate seconds, gauging her chances of escape. Then she moved, sliding across the seat, putting her foot on the wheel-hub.

And then, while she could feel her heart pounding with the excitement of it, she heard the shots—two of them—from inside the cabin. She froze utterly still, facing the cabin, the strength and courage draining out of her.

Cardowan appeared at the door in the act of holstering his gun, a rope in his other hand.

"Drive the team over to the corral," he ordered her curtly, and set out for the corral himself.

Kate brought the horses to life and drove the buckboard over to the corral. She wanted to ask questions, to know what had gone on inside the shack, but she knew without having to ask. Cardowan had decoyed the man into the shack on some pretense, made sure that the homesteader lived alone, then shot him.

As if to answer her unspoken question, Cardowan looked down at her as he climbed the corral poles.

"There's more than one way to settle with an unreasonable man," he said carelessly. "He wouldn't sell me his horses."

That was all. Kate sat there, fear rising up in her like a wave of nausea, until Cardowan's voice dragged her attention to him.

"I said to unhitch that team. We're packing out of here."

It took him a surprisingly short time to rope two of the sturdier horses. He packed the *aparejos* on them, then went into the shed and brought out a saddle. He roped a chunky sorrel next, threw the saddle on him, then mounted to top him off. The horse was gentle, and he grunted with pleasure. There was a long-legged black watching in the corner of the corral, and now Cardowan singled him out and put a loop over him. This was a different proposition. The black fought, but Cardowan went at it just as he had gone about mastering the team.

He snubbed the black to a corral pole, got a hackamore over his head, then yanked the tieknot loose, vaulted on his back and proceeded to top him off. The horse fought savagely, plunging and screaming and pitching, but Cardowan rode him with that ruthless quiet determination that was almost ponderous in its stubbornness.

When the black gave up, Cardowan trotted him over to Kate. "In the saddle. We're riding."

He led off through the timber, still heading south along a cattle trail. Kate was hungry, but the thought of escape was no longer in her mind. Cardowan had seen to it that she got a slower horse, and she suspected that part of his exhibition of riding there in the corral was to show her how little chance of success any attempt at escape would have with him.

The riding took some of the chill off the early-morning air, but there was a hard core of cold fear in Kate that would not thaw out. Again and again she tried to tell herself that this was too impossible, that Cardowan could not hope to make the border safely, but then she remembered how he shaped events for himself and she knew he would succeed.

When the trail they were traveling petered out, Cardowan struck out blind through the sparse timber that was giving way to the cedar-stippled sandhills. Kate was settling down into a fog of weariness when Cardowan pulled up and waited for her.

They were on a low ridge that sloped down a sandy hillside to the thread of railroad track far below. A line of telegraph poles paralleled it. A half mile down the track, a red-painted and scaffolded water tank raised its gaunt skeleton beside the rails.

Cardowan looked at the sun and announced, "We're in plenty of time."

"Yes," Kate said dully.

"You'll like it across the border," Cardowan continued, as if he had allowed her time enough to let the knowledge of her new life sink in. "They know me in Mexico. There'll be no running from hide-out to hide-out down there."

Without waiting for her reply, he nosed his horse down the slope.

They pulled up at the water tank, and while Kate sought its cool shade Cardowan removed the packs from the horses, herded them together and drove them back up the slope. He returned on foot a few minutes later and sat down under the tank. He listened to the monotonous drip of the water, which was seeping through the board tank and dripping down to the cinders, while he rolled a cigarette and lighted it.

Then he fixed his cold gaze on Kate, who was sitting stiffly on the packs. "Come here, sister," he drawled pleasantly, and added, "The name's Kate, isn't it?"

She said nothing, staring at him with wide eyes. She did not move. He removed the cigarette from his mouth and regarded her with an appraising and critical eye.

"It won't be long before you learn I mean what I say," he drawled ominously. When she still did not move, he said curtly, "Come here!"

She rose and walked over to him.

"Sit down!"

She sat tailor fashion beside him, keeping her glance steadily on the horizon and her face was stiff and lifeless. He reached out and touched her hair. "That's what I like about you," he said judiciously. "That hair. I'll leave these black-haired greasers for the others. Me, I savvy blond women best."

Kate did not even wince under his coarseness, but she could not help flinching when he touched her. He noticed it and laughed and let his hand fall to his side.

"Still expecting help, Kate?"

"No. But I can still hope," she answered in a low, bitter voice.

He tapped his chest with curved forefinger and said

quietly. "Don't. I've never met the man yet that could take the woman I wanted away from me. You're with me until I throw you away."

"Poco St. Vrain could have," she answered.

He dropped the cigarette and sat up. As always, that name made him uneasy.

He said, "Listen. You saw what happened to that saddle-tramp there at the mine when he crossed me, didn't you?"

"Yes. I helped him up from the canyon."

Cardowan's eyes narrowed. "You did, huh? And did he tell you his name? He must have."

"Of course."

Cardowan said slowly, "You aren't expecting him to help you. He's over on the other side of the mountains wondering where the gold is gone."

"He wouldn't help me if he was here. But he would kill you."

Cardowan said contemptuously. "He's bogus. He hasn't the guts or the brains to take you or this gold from me."

Kate's blue eyes turned upon him. "That's what I told him. That's why I'm sure he'll meet up with you sooner or later."

Cardowan shrugged and smiled narrowly. "I'll make it later—after you've been with me a while." He cuffed his hat back and yawned, but he watched her closely. "You don't believe I can get away with it?" he asked suddenly.

"No."

Cardowan rose and said, "Come along."

They walked down the tracks perhaps a quarter of a mile. Then Cardowan looked up at the telegraph wires curving from pole to pole both ways as far as sight lasted. He flipped up his gun, cocked it, paused only long enough to steady it and shot. The wire snapped next to an insulator, and whipped down to the ground.

"That's the first precaution," he announced, turning to her. "When the train stops for water, we'll board it, gold and all. You won't talk to anyone"—and here his voice got more ominously gentle—"will you?"

Kate did not answer.

"Because if you do it'll just make a little more work for me. But I don't think you will," he continued softly. "I've got a habit of working contrariness out of a woman, just like I do a horse. Get what I mean?"

Kate nodded dully in assent.

"This track goes east a good many miles, turns north again to rim the desert and joins the main line up here a hundred miles or so. We'll drop off before we hit the junction, cut the wires on the main line, board the train and we'll swing farther east and south almost as far as the border. It'll be easy from there on."

Pathetically easy, Kate thought. No one could catch their train. There would be no way to send the news either. It was as if the railroad had been invented and developed for just this occasion and this use. And again she thought of Poco St. Vrain, could almost see him smile crookedly and say, "Sure, the world and everything in it is made for those bold enough to take it."

She turned back, Cardowan beside her. The sun overhead was brassy and unpitying, and its heat made her lightheaded, unable to think and not even wanting to. When they were close to the tank again, Cardowan paused and put out a hand to detain her.

"Listen," he said. He felt by the rail and put his ear almost on it. Even she could hear the singing in it.

He rose and said, "It's coming."

He did not speak again until they were under the water tank. Then he said, "Get this straight. I'm ranching up in the mountains. You're my wife. I sunk a hole on our land and this stuff is samples I'm taking in to have assayed in Silver City. You're going along for your health, and for the trip. That's really why we're going. This sample stuff is just damfoolery that I feel kinda sheepish about. Our name is O'Brien. We're new to the country. You're Kate. I'm Curt. Don't talk. Sleep a lot. You'll sit with me and I'll go through considerable fuss to see you're comfortable. A neighboring homesteader drove us down here. And I'll do the talking. You got all that?"

Kate said she had.

Cardowan rammed the single empty out of the chamber of his gun, put a fresh load in, then carried the sacks out on the right-of-way up the track a ways.

She could see the train now, snaking into view around the bend up the tracks. It's black plume of smoke from the diamond-shaped stack washed back over the two cars —baggage and passenger.

It pulled in with a gigantic clatter of raw steel on steel, of screaming, bucking brakes. Cardowan waved genially to the engineer and then the high-cabbed locomotive rolled past them and jarred to a stop.

A scattering of smoke-grimed and travel-weary passengers alighted from the coach to stretch. They were mostly ranchers, some traveling men in city clothes, strangely out of place in this country. An old woman was assisted out by a tall gangly puncher, who appeared to be her son. Some of the men, invariably ranchers in cow-boots, walked stiff-legged down to the tank and doused their heads in the dripping water.

Cardowan, nodding pleasantly to anybody who noticed them, murmured, "Stick with me."

The brakie, in stiff blue gold-braided cap, was in shirt-sleeves on the rear platform.

Cardowan walked up to him and passed the time of day while he pulled out money for the two fares. Then he said, "Mind if I load some stuff on the platform here?"

The brakie said he didn't.

Again Cardowan picked up the gold and heaved one tarp-covered load of it on the railed-in platform, and then the other.

"Whatever that is, it's dang heavy," the brakie observed shrewdly. He was a wizened little man with sharp eyes, his cheek bulged by a wad of chew. He had that belly-out, legs-spread stance peculiar to men who live on the sea and on trains.

Cardowan grinned and said, "Samples. Taking them up to Silver City."

"You don't look like no prospector," the brakie offered

without a trace of self-consciousness at his frank curiosity.

"I'm a cowman," Cardowan said, "but I aim to pull out of it as soon as I know my way around with ore."

"What do you aim to do with your wife?" the brakie asked and laughed. Kate, who had been standing silently watching this play, flushed at the knowledge that already she was being accepted as this killer's woman.

"I'm takin' her up to leave her with a doctor upstate."

The brakie nodded sagely, as if he were used to seeing sick women and understood the frailty of the sex.

Cardowan and the brakie gossiped the few minutes left while the tender drank in water from the tank spout. The passengers filed back into the car. When they were all aboard, Cardowan helped Kate up the steps and they entered the car. Cardowan chose a seat which had a vacant neighbor before and behind, and Kate sat next the wall. The train bucked to a start and they were underway.

Kate leaned back against the hard and dirty red-plush seat and closed her eyes, tired in mind and body and weary of trying to think her way out of this.

She did not know how long she had slept, but when she awoke, it was with a sense that much time had passed. For a moment she lay utterly still, her head turned toward the aisle. Suddenly she was aware that Cardowan was not sitting beside her. Slowly, imperceptibly, she opened one eye, and saw that across the aisle and down two seats Cardowan was sitting with three other men in a poker game. He was facing her, sitting next the aisle, and every now and then he looked up at her.

Behind her a man coughed, and she heard him stir in his seat and blow his nose.

She closed her eyes and shifted a little lower in the seat, as a person will in sleep. When her hand touched the seat, it covered a neat pile of burned matches which Cardowan had placed beside him instead of throwing them on the floor. Kate resisted the impulse to open her eyes and look at them, but soon her feeling told her what they were.

And with that knowledge something started clicking in her brain. She fought it, but it would not go. For many long minutes she sat there relaxed, her eyes shut, listening to the murmur of the card players ahead, the droning click of the wheels and the creaking lurch of the car, mingled with subdued murmur of conversation. But she was building something carefully in her mind, weighing the chances.

Finally she opened her eyes a little, and looked at Cardowan. He was talking with the man next him, while one of the players dealt. Kate reckoned that only her head would be visible to Cardowan above the seat ahead of her. She remembered a note which was in her skirt pocket, a note she had scribbled to McCandless there in the hotel, and which the clerk refused to deliver. Slowly now, her eyes still shut, she drew it out.

She picked up the handful of burnt matches, and using one as a pencil so long as the carbon on it lasted, then discarding it for a fresh one, she wrote, her eyes shut, on the back of the note: The man with me is Espey Cardowan, outlaw. Tell the brakeman and take him. There is a reward.

Finished, she opened her eyes enough to read what she had written. Some of it was faint, but the matches had scored the paper deeply enough so that if it were read carefully it was understandable. And now she hesitated, wondering if the man behind her was able to read, or if he would be one of the traveling men, gunless, sceptical, who would prefer to mind his own business.

She kept the note long enough to mark out her writing to McCandless with the rest of the matches, then she spread it out flat and lowered it through the crack in the seat, holding on to the tip of it, and pulled it back and forth and sideways, hoping its movement would attract the attention of the man behind her.

It was a long minute, a minute spent in covertly watching Cardowan look up at her, then at his cards, before she was rewarded. The note was taken from her hand.

And now, her eyes opened just the slightest, she watched Cardowan. He looked up at her, then away, then suddenly his gaze shuttled up again, past her this time.

She saw him move as if to get up, heard a scuffling of feet behind her, then Cardowan lunged erect, his hand whipping to his hip, streaking up in a tight invisible arc that ended in a flash of orange and a roar.

It whipped by her face, and the thud of it on flesh, the strangled scream of the man behind her, and his falling body, all came at once as Cardowan leaped across the aisle to a standing position on the opposite seat and covered the car with his outspread guns. Men rose, and looked into his guns and stood utterly still, a look of bewilderment on their faces.

"Stand against the windows, the lot of you!" Cardowan whipped out. "This is a stick-up!"

The dozen men in the car obeyed.

Cardowan said to him without taking his moving gaze from the armed ranchers, "Come over here, brakie."

The brakie came over.

"Take every one of their guns out and drop them on the floor. One mismove and you'll get it in the back!"

Kate watched with held breath as the brakie moved down the short length of the car and disarmed every man there.

"Now step out into the aisle and walk to the rear of the coach!" Cardowan said loudly. "One at a time."

The men filed out into the aisle, looking angry, and walked to the end of the car. Even the old lady got up and hobbled down the aisle. When they were all past, Cardowan said to Kate, "You too, sister."

She got up, and glanced at the man behind her slumped in a pool of blood on the seat. He was a puncher, dressed in Levis, the hand holding his Colt lying peacefully across his chest, a ragged hole in his face under his eye that was running a thin stream of blood down his cheek.

As she passed up the aisle Cardowan drawled, "I told you it would only make trouble if you did it."

And Kate, numb with the misery and knowledge that she had caused a man's death, bowed her head.

When she reached the huddled passengers in the rear of the coach, Cardowan said:

"Now open that door and the lot of you get out on the platform. You too, sister."

Someone started to protest, and Cardowan shot into the floor at Kate's feet. "Get out!"

The door was opened and the dozen men and two women crowded out onto the rear platform.

Cardowan stood in the door, both guns leveled, and said curtly, "Now, over you go. One at a time. Don't try to swing up on the roof and don't stall. I'd rather shoot you!"

"But, you damned scoundrel!" the brakie exploded. "We'll break our legs!"

"Would you rather get shot?" Cardowan drawled easily, and swiveled a gun to the brakie in one corner.

For three long seconds the brakie looked him in the eye, then he said quietly, "Yes."

On the heel of his word Cardowan let his left gun off. The brakie tried to cough, strangled on it, then slumped down into a sitting position on the platform. The old woman moaned. Kate looked at Cardowan, her face drawn in horror, but Cardowan only smiled.

"Who else?" he drawled.

"I'll go over," one man said. "But may God rot your foul soul, you black-hearted bastard!"

This man climbed the rail, holding onto the braking wheel, while the others watched. He waited a few seconds until the right-of-way was a little less steep, then he leaped to the side. His body plummeted off, hit the slope, and rolled over and over and down in a moil of dust.

Everyone watched him. He struggled to his feet and waved encouragement to the others.

"Next," Cardowan said briefly.

The others followed, some leaping clear of the sleepers, others, the heavier men especially, leaping off awkwardly and not getting up when they had finished the long roll to the land level below. But one by one, cursing Cardowan, they went over.

At last there was only the puncher, a solemn-faced young man burned to mahogany, with flashing black eyes, and his old mother standing beside Kate.

The puncher said, "Are you going to make her jump?"

"After you, mister," Cardowan drawled coolly.

"Then you'll shoot us both," the old woman said staunchly. She was a frail old lady, dressed in a full black dress and a black bonnet. Her face was wrinkled, drawn and carved in those deep lines that a frontier bred in its women, but in her eyes was a fearless courage that would not quail before Cardowan's guns.

Cardowan started to raise his gun obligingly when Kate cried, "You can't, you can't! Oh, don't you see what you're doing! Don't kill her! She can't harm you, can't stop you from doing what you want!"

"She was going over to a doctor because her broken leg hadn't knit good," the puncher said sturdily. "She can't jump. It would kill her."

Kate said, "Oh, please, please leave her!"

"You better shoot," the puncher said. He put his arm around the old lady and drew her to him.

Cardowan hesitated, his face unsmiling. Then he shrugged and twisted his mouth into a meager smile. "All right, old woman. You can stay on. But your son either jumps or gets shot."

"Jump, son," the old lady said quickly. "I'll be all right. Nothing will happen to me."

The boy's tortured face turned to her, asking a wordless question.

"I know," the old lady said. "I'll be all right. I can't harm him. You jump—and jump good."

The boy's bleak gaze settled on Cardowan and he said hoarsely, "If you harm her, you'll never find the hide-out I can't reach."

"Go on, please," Kate told him quickly. "Go on!"

The puncher squeezed his mother's arm, climbed the rail, went over to the side, waited a moment, then leaped clear. He rolled down the long grade in a funnel of dust and rock, but at the bottom he was on his feet. He waved to them, and watched till the train pulled out of sight around a bend.

Cardowan said, "Come inside now and sit on the end seat, both of you."

They watched him pick up the guns from the floor and fling them through the windows. When his inspection was finished he passed them and went out to the rear platform. At the tarp-wrapped bundles with their dusty footprints of the men who had stood on them as they climbed the rail, he only cast a casual glance.

Then he searched the pockets of the brakie for keys. He found none, so he dumped the body over the rail and did not even watch it pitch down the bank like a sack of loose oats.

Inside he found the brakie's coat, and in the side pocket were keys. He took them, saying, "Stay here. I'm going up front."

As a matter of precaution he locked the front door of the car, swung across the link coupling, and switching the Colt to his left hand softly tried the door to the baggage car. It was locked. Bracing himself against the sway of the car, he tried key after key, inserting it softly so as to make no noise. He tried many before he found the right one, and then he turned the lock softly, and waited. Nothing happened.

Now he drew his other gun, held it in his hand and reached for the doorknob, twisted it, then flung his weight against it. The door flew open and he leaped inside.

The baggage car, beside a litter of bundles on the floor, contained a wall rack for mailsacks, a waysafe, a waist-high wall desk, a shelf of pigeonholes reaching from floor to ceiling, two chairs—and two men, who were both sitting down.

They looked at Cardowan indifferently, thinking him the brakeman, but when they saw the guns they rose slowly, the light from the window showing their faces as they paled. Cardowan walked over to them and said, "Howdy, boys."

"I'll open that waysafe," one of them offered. "There ain't nothin' in it but change."

"Don't bother," Cardowan said mildly, looking around

the car. He spotted the shotgun leaning against the desk and maneuvered around so that he was between it and the men. Then he flipped their guns out on the floor and said, "Go into the coach."

They obeyed. He prodded them through it, past Kate and the old lady, out onto the back platform, and said, "Jump."

By now, both men knew what had happened. Grim-faced, cursing him, they went over the end. Again he did not even bother to see whether they made it or not.

Then he came back into the car, closed the door, and stood in the aisle looking down at Kate and the old woman. Slowly he holstered his guns.

"Step out here, sister," he drawled slowly.

Kate stood up and faced him, her chin firm, her eyes hard with loathing.

"You gave him a note, was that it?"

"Yes."

"You didn't understand, then, what I meant when I said I didn't like contrariness in a woman?"

"I understood," Kate said coldly. "Do you think you could do anything to me that would make me feel worse than watching you murder people, torturing them?"

"I wonder now if I could," Cardowan drawled, his eyes getting narrower. "Anyway, I could try."

He brought his open hand around in a long arc that smacked against Kate's cheek like a whiplash. She fell into the seat, and slowly raised her hand to her face. She did not cry out, and there were no tears in her eyes as she looked up at him. The blow hurt, stunned her a little, but she would have died rather than show it.

He put a hand on the seat rail and leaned over her.

"When I say I break horses like I do women, I mean it. Understand?"

"Perfectly."

Again he slapped her, this time across the mouth, so that her lip was beat into her teeth and the salt taste of blood filled her mouth. She did not whimper.

"Don't make any mistake about me," Cardowan

drawled coldly, leaning over her. "Man, beast or woman, I can break them. And a woman is just about the easiest."

And as if to give her a reminder, he slapped her again.

Cardowan stood erect now, hands in belt, and watched her, smiling.

Then he looked at the old woman, who was watching him with eyes no longer gentle.

"That's the way to treat 'em, old lady. You might have raised a man for a son instead of a mamma's boy if your old man had given you a little of that."

The old lady said nothing. Cardowan waited to see if she would, and when she didn't, he laughed silently, lounged into the seat across the aisle, built a cigarette, and yawned while he did it.

He had forgotten Kate already, now that his first lesson to her was over. And the train, as if oblivious to everything that had gone on, beat its racketing way through the hot sunshine, its pall of cinders and smoke just as acrid, just as black, and it went just as fast—away from all help.

CHAPTER TWENTY

WHEN THEY HIT the upgrade of the San Jons, Harry settled into a sort of an irritable coma. He knew he couldn't hurry the horses, knew he would have to let them take their own time if he was to get anything out of them later.

Poco chafed under it too, but he knew that if his scheme was to have a chance to work, he would have to be patient, and patient in the teeth of what he knew was happening to Kate Shayne.

Van saw the somber look on his face and said, "You're bound to lose, St. Vrain. You can't win all the time."

"I found that out. I'll win this time, though."

They were close to the pass, moving at a snail's pace, when the stage stopped and Poco heard the brakes set.

He stuck his head out the window and said, "What's up, Harry?"

Harry swore bitterly. "The damned army. I think I seen

'em up ahead." He leaned down and said glumly, "I heard about that sandy you run on 'em over to Benjamin. If they see you there'll be hell to pay."

Poco said, "Tell 'em I'm here if they stop us—and they will."

Harry scowled.

"I figured on this. Let me play it my own way, Harry, will you?"

"Sure," Harry said, puzzled.

"Then throw down one of Van's six-guns."

Harry obeyed, Poco drew back into the stage as it started again and sat down, and proceeded to plug every load out of the gun Harry had given him. Then he gave the gun to Van, who accepted it, watching him curiously.

"The army's coming," Poco said calmly. "They'll likely stop to get the news about the fight in Rincon. You hail them. Tell them how we got away, and that you were coming out this way to meet them just in case the posse took after us. We were heading for Benjamin for army protection. You got that?"

"Sure," Van said slowly, puzzled.

"You've got that gun there guarding me. It's empty, but they won't notice that. "This"—he tapped his own gun—"won't be empty. And Sam Van," he continued in a soft, lifeless voice, "it will be empty, all five slugs buried in you, if you give me away. Have you got that—really got it? Because if you cross me now I'll turn into the killer you say I'm not."

Van's wise eyes narrowed. He knew when a man was serious, had recognized before that back-to-the-wall tone of desperation in a man's voice. He did now. He said, "Yes, I've got it."

"This won't be an escape," Poco said. "I'll give you my word for that. Only I don't want the army around me. They're reasonable men, but they've got orders to capture me and take me back to Benjamin. I'm not going."

"You've chosen a damned funny way to dodge them," Van observed dryly. "You're walking right into them."

"And I'll walk right out. There'll likely be an officer in

charge of the outfit. We'll stop and you'll talk, invite him inside, so you can give him your story while we're riding. Tell him to tie his horse on behind. That'll be all you'll need to do."

Van said, "And you say this won't be an escape?"

"It'll look like it," Poco said slowly, grimly, "but it won't be. You'll have me tonight. If you don't capture me, I'll give you my word to give myself up. I said my word. Does that suit you?"

Van said, "I've heard about that word of yours. You keep it, don't you?"

"Yes. That's what I'm doing now—keeping my word, to somebody I gave it to a long time back."

"A woman?"

"A lady," Poco corrected gently, and added, "A mighty pretty lady that hates me and everything I do and everything I stand for. That's why I want to keep it, why I've got to keep it." He looked at Van. "Will you do it?"

"I haven't any choice," Van replied. "You've got the loaded gun."

Poco said, "You understand a lot of things, Sam Van, but you can't understand why I'm doing it this way. I think you want to help me, but if there was no gun to threaten you, you'd feel it was your duty to stop me, wouldn't you?"

Van smiled and nodded.

"So I'm not making you give your word," Poco continued gently. "I'm threatening you—and I'll carry it out if you cross me."

His dark unblinking eyes sought Van's and there was a question in his face. Van looked out the window, then said, without turning to him, "I can't buck an armed man with an empty gun, can I?"

Poco smiled. "Thanks," he said. "I don't want to kill you."

He took his gun and rammed it in the waistband of his Levis in the small of his back, then leaned back in the seat. Their positions were changed now, and it was Van who appeared to be the captor.

They rode this way until they heard the drumming of approaching horses, and Harry pulled up and set the brake.

Van leaned out and waved, and suddenly the stage was surrounded by cavalry troopers.

"Howdy, Lieutenant," Van said amiably, holding out the marshal's badge.

"Hello, Marshal," the officer answered slowly. "Hell, I thought you sent over for—"

"I did. But we made a getaway. Take a look inside."

The lieutenant rode close to the stage and looked inside at Poco, who raised a lazy hand in greeting.

Lieutenant Cooper nodded briefly and smiled. "Nice work, Marshal."

Van said, "There's likely a posse after us now, Lieutenant, so your trip wasn't wasted. What happened to the man I sent over?"

"He nearly killed his horse and himself. He's at the barracks. He said they were holding you up in the jail when he left. How'd you make your getaway?"

Van laughed, "It's a long story. Tie your horse on behind here and come inside. I'll tell you."

Instead of doing this, Cooper dismounted and handed the reins of his long-legged chestnut gelding over to one of his men. Poco looked long at this horse, noted the long slim legs, the small intelligent head, the long neck, the coiled muscles playing under the sheen of its coat. The horse was breathing hard, and he noticed that, too.

The lieutenant removed his gauntlets, tucked them in his belt, climbed inside and took the seat opposite Van and Poco, after telling the men to follow behind.

Van leaned out, shouted, "Let her roll," to Harry, and the stage started its slow course to the top of the grade not far distant now.

Cooper, his thin face smiling slightly, studied Poco with unfeigned interest.

"You've done a bad thing, my man," he said quietly. "We don't let every outlaw ride up to a government fort and shoot at the flag."

Poco yawned and said nothing.

Cooper turned to Van. "Well, how'd you do it?"

Van launched into his story and told it word for word. At the mention of Cardowan and Two-Way slugging him in jail, Cooper stopped him. "Those two prospectors? Why would they do that?"

When Van looked puzzled at the question Cooper explained that Two-Way and Cardowan were prospectors who sought shelter from Poco's gang in Fort Benjamin. Van told him the truth, that Two-Way and Cardowan were crooks, who had hoodwinked the commandant.

"But you were chasing them, weren't you?" Cooper asked Poco.

"All this will be straightened out soon," Poco drawled in a bored voice. He hoped the chestnut gelding was blowing himself thoroughly. Cooper looked at him, puzzled, but Van took up the story, telling of their escape.

They had reached the top of the grade now, and as soon as they passed through a long level stretch they would hit the other slope.

Cooper was saying, "That was lucky," just as Poco arched his back, as if to scratch it, and whipped out a six-gun, cocked, and pointed it at Cooper.

Cooper's voice trailed off into silence. He stared at Poco, then at Van.

"It was a trick, Lieutenant," Van said, holding up his own gun. "Mine's empty. St. Vrain wanted to toll you in here."

"I see," Cooper said quietly. "You might have told me when the men had surrounded the stage."

"He'd of got five slugs in his back if he did," Poco put in. "You'll get the five instead unless you do what I say."

"And what's that?"

Poco said, "I'm going to borrow your horse."

Cooper said nothing.

Poco continued, "Van will call up for Harry to stop. When your men get even with us, lean out the window and tell them to fall back a half mile or so. Tell them there's likely a posse on our trail and you want the prisoner kept out of the row, if there is one. Also, tell them to leave your horse, to tie it on the back end."

"And if I don't?" Cooper drawled.

"You will," Poco said gently, ominously. "I busted out of your fort. I'll bust loose from your men. Besides, I'll give myself up to you tonight."

"Sure," Cooper said dryly. "You take my horse, so you can ride around and get some fresh air before you surrender."

"He will," Van said simply. "Take his word for it."

Poco shifted the gun to his other hand closest the side wall, and laid it between his leg and the wall.

"All right, Van. Stop Harry."

Van leaned out and yelled up to him.

The stage rumbled to a stop and Poco said to Cooper, "I don't like heroes, Lieutenant. A dead hero only gets mentioned in an army citation. A live one that talks an outlaw into surrendering gets a promotion. I'll surrender to you and Van tonight and you'll get the credit."

"Where?"

"You'll chase me. It'll be where I let you overtake me," Poco said arrogantly.

By now the troopers were pulling up even with the stage. Cooper took a long level look at Poco, who smiled narrowly, then leaned out the window.

"They tell me there's a posse following, Sergeant," Cooper said. "Drop back with your men. Stop the posse, inform them that the prisoner is being taken to the fort. Don't fight. If they insist on seeing for themselves, ride down to us. We'll keep on. And leave my horse, Sergeant. Tie him to the rear."

"Right, sir," the sergeant said, and added, "You better watch out, sir. That St. Vrain's tricky."

Cooper smiled faintly and said, "Yes, he is, isn't he?"

The sergeant led the chestnut up, tied him, then Poco heard him ordering the troopers to turn around.

Poco said, "Tell Harry to roll her."

Van did. The stage groaned into motion again. As soon as it was around the first bend in the road Poco ordered

Van to tell Harry to pull up.

When the stage stopped, Poco prodded Cooper and Van out into the road. Harry chuckled softly at the sight, and Poco grinned back at him.

"Want to come along, Harry?" Poco asked. "We can cut a horse out and you'll have a chance in the hills."

"Huh-uh," Harry said, "I'll stick it out, Poco. They ain't got a thing on me except leavin' a gun in the seat."

"That'll be several years," Van put in.

"*If* you can prove I done it a-purpose. *If* you can prove I left it there a-tall. I been with this outfit ten years. They'll stick by me."

"I hope they will," Van said. "You need them."

Poco led the chestnut around and looked him over.

"Nice horse. I'd rather ride bareback, though, than keep that saddle. Rip it off, Cooper."

The lieutenant did. Poco then took the gun from Cooper's side holster and threw it up in the grass. He thought he detected a gleam of amusement in Cooper's eyes when he handed the horse over to him.

"He's a good horse," Cooper said. "Treat him well."

Poco only smiled and led the horse up the road. Then he holstered his gun, seized the mane of the chestnut in his hands and, while he skipped and danced away from him, vaulted on. He turned and waved his hand.

Only then did Cooper have sense enough to run off the road for his gun. Harry was already sawing the stage around at Van's orders to go back for the troopers.

Poco smiled and pulled his hat down tighter. The chestnut had a long and tireless lope, unjarring, effortless, and he was a willing worker and seemed to love the run.

The army horses had almost blotted out the tracks of the buckboard, but now and again they showed in the dust of the road. Poco watched them all the way down the slope, and when he saw them turn off into the sideroad in the foothills, he pulled up.

It didn't take more than simple logic to interpret this move on Cardowan's part. The closest railroad point was several miles along the foothills to the spot where the train pulled over the pass and down the slope. It took on water there. Cardowan and Kate could have boarded her there.

Poco recalled the route. He knew the track led straight east for many miles, then dived down into the badlands that bordered the desert, turned south once it had dropped two thousand feet and rimmed the desert in a twisting, dodging effort to avoid the canyons on one hand and the sand drifts of the desert on the other. It kept north for miles doing this, climbing a little, too. Then, just before it came to the spur that led to Christian City, it made the pass that it was laboring toward the whole afternoon.

Poco looked at the sun. Close to noon. He had till almost dark to make that pass. It meant crossing miles of San Jons benchland, skirting Fort Benjamin, and taking a few miles off the badlands—all before sunset, the time the train usually pulled into the pass. He had a good horse, an easy trail—and the knowledge that if he did not reach Kate Shayne by sundown, he would be too late. The army would trail him and so would the posse. If he made it in time, he would get the gold, return it to her, kill Cardowan and give himself up.

"All because I met a girl," He reflected quietly. "A girl who thinks I'm just a killer—and a man who thinks I'm not."

CHAPTER TWENTY-ONE

I T WAS PAST NOON when Cardowan began to get sleepy. The train had sloped down off the San Jons bench into the deep and dark canyons of the broken country, snaking along the bottom of gorges whose walls almost shut out the light of day.

Kate and the old lady—Mrs. Baily was her name, Kate learned by whispered conversation—sat utterly still, too frightened to sleep, and afraid to talk. Kate watched Cardowan, her eyes smoldering. His striking her did not humiliate her; it only served to feed the fury and hate and fear that was in her. She watched him nod and almost doze, only to catch himself and open his eyes again.

Finally, when he knew that sleep was inevitable, he lounged to his feet and swayed against the rocking of the train.

"Come along with me, both of you," he commanded.

He led the way into the baggage car, and while Kate and the old lady looked on, hunted the car through for any kind of weapon. He found only what he had known before was there: the shotgun, the two Colts shucked out by the baggagemen. These he took and said, "You can't get out, so don't try."

Going out, he locked the solid door behind him, and went on through the car, lay down and was immediately asleep.

Kate watched the door long after he had left.

"He's mad," Mrs. Baily said calmly. "Who is he?"

Kate told her, told the whole horrible story.

"You poor child," Mrs. Baily said in a hushed voice. "Isn't there any chance for help at all? Doesn't anybody know you're gone?"

"One man," Kate said quietly. "He knows."

"Does he love you, child?" Mrs. Baily asked calmly.

Kate shook her head and said bitterly, "He hates me. He wants the gold."

"Ah," Mrs. Baily said.

Kate wanted to throw herself into the old woman's arms and cry, but something inside her would not let her. She smiled crookedly. "Let's try to sleep. We're safe until he wakes, at least."

Kate threw some of the mail sacks on the floor, and hard as they were, Mrs. Baily was asleep as soon as she lay down. Kate was only seconds later.

She wakened late in the afternoon, and for a moment she lay there, wondering where she was, and then the knowledge bore down on her with its weight of sorrow.

She rose, leaving the old woman asleep, and walked over to one of the barred windows.

The train was going slow now, winding its way through this tortured land, climbing imperceptibly. Even if she could break these bars now, she still could not escape, she thought wearily. There was Mrs. Baily whom she could not leave. She couldn't even guess what Cardowan would do to the old woman if he came back and found Kate gone. She shuddered involuntarily.

But the thought of staying here, submitting to this man like a helpless sheep, angered her as much as it frightened her. She called up all those things her father had said about men, about believing good of them, being fair with them, and she smiled crookedly at the thought. Poor Dad. He had never known men like Cardowan, nor their deeds and crimes. Something balled up in her throat when she thought of him. McCandless could take his vengeance now on the careless manager of his mine, and there would be no one to back her father up, to comfort him, to help bear his troubles. Instead, his daughter would be the cheap woman of a notorious killer.

She turned away, sick at heart, but her mind was made up. She would try to escape and take Mrs. Baily with her, even if it meant death. So she started a methodical search of the car. On top the shelf of pigeonholes she found a paper-wrapped parcel of lunch left by the baggagemen. But that wasn't what she was looking for. It was a gun, anything to kill. Her mind would not form that word, for she hated it, but it was there, unspoken, but thought. A search of the car revealed nothing that might help her, so she started opening the few bundles of freight that remained. In one canvas-wrapped bundle, probably the outfit of a prospector, she found a handax.

Picking it up, she settled back on her heels, looking at it. If she hid behind the door as Cardowan came in, raised the ax and— No. That wasn't the way. No matter how desperate she was it was impossible to do that. The train was laboring mightily now, and as she listened to the slow rhythm of the clicking wheels they seemed to say, "Do it, do it, do it!"

She knelt there a long time, fighting it, listening to the wheels, looking around the dark baggage car, thinking of her hatred for Cardowan, and lastly, thinking *if* she was going to do it, how she would go about it.

And then the train seemed to pull out of the canyon walls and the low light of the sun flooded the car. She shivered a bit and stood up. The train increased its speed now, as if it were on the downgrade. No, she reflected, she couldn't do it. But the ax might be of use. She laid it behind the door, and went back to the mail sacks.

As she sat down, she heard the brakes being applied gently, and felt the train slow up, then come to a stop. She rose again now, and went to the west window of the car. They seemed to be lying in the bottom of a broad rocky valley running east and west. Stretching out toward the west down the valley, she saw a spur of the track at right angles to them vanish behind rocks in the distance. She had no knowledge where she was, but she judged they had come a considerable distance that day, since the sun was just lowering over the high skyline to the west and the country held that evening stillness that was accentuated by the lack of train noises. Opening the window, she could hear the slow breathing of the engine ahead with its accompanying clanking.

What did it mean? Were they taking on more water? Surely the engine crew would notice the absence of any passengers and become suspicious. She felt her heart pounding inside her. If Cardowan killed the engine crew in one of his whims, perhaps help would come to them.

But she heard no sound out there. Suddenly, there was a blast from the engine's whistle, and then silence again, and for a long time. She listened, waiting. Mrs. Baily came up now and listened with her.

"What is it?"

"I don't know. I haven't heard gunshots."

As her voice died out, she heard the crunch of a man walking on cinders. He passed beneath them and Kate, remembering her last attempt to get help, stifled the impulse to call out.

Suddenly, the crunching stopped.

"Howdy," Cardowan's voice said amiably. He was standing on the platform between the two cars.

"Where's everybody?" a strange voice said. Kate guessed it must belong to one of the engine crew.

"Who's everybody?" Cardowan drawled quietly. She could almost picture him leaning against the end of the car, thumbs hooked in belt, his face cold, watchful, almost amiable.

"The brakie. The passengers."

"What do you want the brakie for?" Cardowan asked.

There was a little pause, and the crew man said, "He's supposed to shut that switch back there."

"You got an anvil in your pants?" Cardowan drawled.

"It ain't my job," the engine man said curtly. "Who the hell—"

There was a whisper of something on leather, and the man's voice trailed off.

"Suppose you make it your job, *hombre*," Cardowan's voice said. "It's a fifty-yard walk back there. I'll make it with you. I need air."

"So those were shots I heard," the engineer said grimly. "The engine makes so much racket I wasn't sure."

"They were shots. Want to hear another?"

"No."

She heard him swing down to the gravel, and the sound of crunching gravel died.

Kate looked at Mrs. Baily.

"Will he shoot him?" the old woman asked.

"I—I don't know," Kate whispered.

She waited until she heard a clank of metal, of the switch being thrown, then she waited again. Presently the sound of cinders crunching underfoot came to her again.

Then voices came within her hearing, but she could not make them out until they were closer.

Cardowan was saying, "—think I'll take a *pasear* up to your engine to see if you've got any irons hid."

The crew man said nothing. They passed under the window. Kate listened some more. In a few seconds the engine started to thrash preliminary to getting under way on the climb up the hill. Cardowan had not come back.

Kate whirled to Mrs. Baily. "I found an ax," she murmured swiftly. "If we can open the door, we may be able to jump off while he's up there!"

"Try it," Mrs. Baily said.

Kate ran across the room, seized the ax, wedged the blade into the crack where the lock was and pried savagely. She worked frantically on it, until her patience gave way and she brought the ax up and chopped down on the lock. Something snapped so loud she could hear it.

Dropping the ax she seized the doorknob and yanked. It flew open.

"Come on!" Kate whispered, and stepped out onto the platform. Mrs. Baily came to the door, took one look at the country passing by them, and shook her head.

"I'd never make it dear, I'm old, and my bones are brittle. You go."

It was a sort of miasmic despair that strangled Kate as she looked at the old woman. It was their only chance for freedom, and they could not take it. Then her eyes fell on the pin and link car coupling. It was a thick link, held in place by two pins which slipped down through solid drawbars from each car, through the link holes, to make the coupling. She stared at it a few seconds and said slowly, "If we could unhook this rear car—"

Mrs. Baily cut in swiftly. "It would roll back down the grade, and turn onto that spur into Christian City. They threw the switch shut!"

Without another word, Kate jumped to the platform of the coach, the second car, knelt and seized the thick head of the pin. Mrs. Baily remained on the baggage car platform, watching. Kate pulled, but her fingers slipped off. The weight of the coach was on the pin, pulling the link against it, and a hundred horses could not have pulled it loose.

They were going through a cut in the rocks now, and suddenly the labor of the train slackened as the grade leveled and the coach drew closer to the baggage car. Mrs. Baily was looking at the coupling, saw it come together.

"Now!" she cried.

Kate seized the pin and pulled. It slipped out easily. She looked up, joy in her face, and then it washed out. The baggage coach on whose platform Mrs. Baily stood was pulling slowly away from the coach on whose platform Kate stood. Mrs. Baily, in her preoccupation, had forgotten to cross over to the coach.

"Jump!" Kate cried.

Mrs. Baily looked and only shook her head. Already it was too late, and the space between the cars had started to grow.

"I can't," she said simply.

Even as she said it, something moved above them. Kate looked up, and in that one brief second, she saw Cardowan leap the distance between the two car roofs. And then they pulled away from each other, the baggage car seeming to speed ahead without the weight of the coach's pull, and the coach stopped and slowly started down the hill.

Kate backed into the door, her breath held, as Cardowan swung down from the overhang, gun in hand.

His face was dark and twisted with fury. He snarled, "You damned meddlesome fool."

Kate's throat was knotted with fear, but Cardowan brushed by her and through the car to the braking wheel on the rear platform.

Holstering his gun, he grasped the wheel and spun it to take up the slack. Already the car was gaining momentum on the downgrade, and the brakes clamped on with a screeching of steel on steel. Cardowan's muscles corded as he threw his weight against the pull, but the car was already speeding. Kate, watching Cardowan now with open mouth, saw the track swing out of sight through the rear door, heard the clack of wheels on the switch, then saw a new and curving track swing into sight.

Cardowan called furiously, "Come here, damn you! and help me!"

And hearing that, Kate knew that she was lost either way, for if she escaped this hurtling and runaway car which had a downgrade for many miles ahead, Cardowan

would turn on her with the insane fury her blunder had
bred in him.

CHAPTER TWENTY-TWO

ACROSS THAT LONG and rolling benchland, Poco could
look back and see for miles. It was early afternoon before
he picked up the long string of dark specks that told him
the army was finally on his trail. But he did not slacken
his speed, nor spur his horse. When he dipped off the
bench into the badlands, he knew they would have a difficult time following him. He knew, too, that he had the
best horse in the lot, and that this chestnut had a reserve
that was not called forth yet.

He bore straight east when he got into the broken
country, threading the maze of canyons, wasting precious
minutes that infuriated him on the incessant switchbacks
and looping stream beds that swung out for a half mile
off the line, then came back almost to the place they
started. But he had no choice. The gravelly arroyos were
the only places he could travel between these sheer and
rocky walls.

And slowly, the sun wheeled overhead, lowering, and
each hour of it he felt his impotence growing and his hope
dimming. He was clinging now, toward that divide and
the pass over which the train would pull.

On a high rockrim in late afternoon, he pulled up and
looked south. He looked for many long minutes, and
finally spotted a smudge of smoke against all that vast and
rocky waste. It would be the train laboring up the long
grade. Panic seized him, but he knew if he lost his head
and started blundering through these canyons at a gallop,
he would either lose his way up some dead-end canyon, or
his horse would founder.

Cursing bitterly he spurred his chestnut on. Already
the canyons were more shallow as they climbed toward
the pass, and he was making better time. But the sun, that
clock which was timing him irrevocably, was lowering,

lowering, and he raged at it and his horse and himself.

Later, much later, the canyons seemed to fall away, and the grade leveled off, and he knew he was almost to the top of this ridge which the pass crossed, but miles to the west of the tracks.

He urged his horse as much as he dared, looking ahead. The sun was already gilding the highest tips of the ridges, and he knew that he had not much time.

And then, when he pulled up on the rim of a deep valley, he looked across it. There, half a mile beyond, he saw the black and red train swing into sight momentarily, as it swung into the cut of the pass. His stomach balled up inside him, and he rammed his spurs into the gelding and shot him down the slope. He was too late, he knew he was too late, but he would try.

He cut up the far slope, achieved the ridge, then slanted down the long slope toward the valley to the north.

Ahead now, a half mile below, he could see the train standing motionless in the cup of the valley. Figures stood by it, but he was too far to distinguish them. They walked back a few yards on the track, paused, then turned to the train.

And then, when he was half way down the slope, he saw the engine labor into motion. It gathered speed slowly, but it was enough.

Poco pulled up his horse and watched it bleakly, and felt hope die within him. Kate Shayne was on that train, and Espey Cardowan had her. For the first time, tasting the galling and bitter impotence of it, he knew that it was not to prove to her that he could be honest that he had done this. It was something more, a strong and wild feeling that he wanted to be with her always, a feeling that hurt more than pain now, that he felt. He turned wearily to look back up the long slope. A few mounted figures were skylined on it. They would be the vanguard of the army, who had followed him all these hours. He would wait here and surrender to them, for he was through. What happened now didn't matter.

He looked off across that wide valley again to the thread

of the railroad track. Everything he ever wanted, ever hoped for, everything that was clean and decent and dependable in his life had vanished there—forever.

But as he looked he saw a railroad coach back through that portal of rocks, coming slowly into sight. Holding his breath, he watched it lumber slowly through and tilt downgrade, gathering speed each second.

And then something exploded in him. He roweled the chestnut savagely and shot down the grade. He let the horse have its head, and watched the car, keeping his seat by instinct. When he saw the coach reach the valley floor, sweep wide in a half circle onto the Christian City spur heading west, he shouted with joy and yanked the chestnut's head, swinging off on the same angle the car was traveling. A man was working at the brake in front.

He gave all his attention to the horse now. He rode with a mad haste and the chestnut, sensing his excitement, caught the madness. He vaulted him over rocks, jumped him off drop-offs, slid him down shale outcrops, and each second he was approaching closer to the point in the valley bottom where he hoped they would meet.

When he finally thundered onto the valley floor, the coach, fifty yards distant, and a little ahead of him, thundered around a curve and out of sight.

The chestnut straightened out into a pumping gallop, and Poco lay low over his neck.

"Take it, boy, take it," Poco prayed. He rounded the bend on the track now and saw the car ahead. He could look clear through its corridor and see two people at the front bending their strength into the braking. And one of them was Kate Shayne, the other Cardowan.

Slowly, as the chestnut let out more and more speed and its muscles were pumping like coiled pistons, Poco saw he was gaining. Inch by inch the chestnut fought, long since past its bottom and running now like any good horse will on guts, and guts alone.

They pulled closer now, smelling the hot smell of metal on metal that came from the squealing brakes. Now the chestnut's head was almost touching the coach end. Poco prayed blindly that Cardowan would not look back.

Then gently, with his knee, he urged the gelding off the ties to the side, and let him run. The chestnut took to the grass-grown right-of-way, which was easier footing, and gained in a long glorious burst of speed. Poco watched, biting his lips. He could not lean far over to catch the platform rail, lest he throw the chestnut off stride—and once that was lost, they were gone. But the gelding forged ahead, each rocking lope gaining an inch. Finally, when Poco could reach out and almost catch the rail, he held his breath and lunged.

He caught the rail with one hand as the horse swerved off to the side. For a moment, Poco dangled by one hand from the rail, then he got his other hand on the grip and pulled himself up.

He sat there a few seconds, getting his breath, loosening his guns in their holsters, feeling the lurching sway of the wild car.

Then he rose and swung through the door. Kate and Cardowan he could see through the corridor, pulling at the brake.

Poco walked down the aisle, softly, swiftly, his hands at his sides. When he reached the rear door, he lounged against its frame and raised his voice, saying,

"Hello, Joker."

Cardowan whirled, along with Kate. Poco wanted to look at her face, to take her in his arms, to tell her everything that had been frozen inside him, but he could not.

"Poco!" Kate cried, and started for him. Suddenly, she checked herself, sensing that she could not go to him yet. She backed off against the siderail, her eyes widening, a cry welling up in her throat.

Cardowan's face was gray, bloodless. He had his back to the rail, and his hands were still on the braking wheel.

Poco said, "Hello, darling."

Kate said nothing, only moaned.

"I'm a killer, Kate," Poco said quietly. "I've come to show you. I'm going to kill Joker here—but it will be the last time I ever draw a gun. You didn't think it was ever necessary. Do you now?"

"Yes," Kate said huskily.

Poco smiled a little, his thin face somber and satanic and utterly expressionless.

He lounged away from the wall now, and caught his balance against the wild sway of the car with widespread feet. He had seen the gold at Cardowan's feet, without even looking at it.

"Joker," he began quietly, "I told you I wouldn't go out of my way to hunt you. I didn't. It wasn't for you I came here. It was for her. Remember?"

Cardowan opened his mouth to speak and no words came.

"But I told you if you ever came within gunshot I'd kill you." He paused. "I'm going to."

Still Cardowan said nothing.

"Any time, Joker. This is payday—the last one," Poco murmured.

He stood utterly relaxed, hands at his sides swaying a little against the lurching car, a terrible smile on his face.

For a moment Cardowan did not move, and then some last remnant of courage flagged him into action. His hands dropped from the wheel. There was five feet between them, five feet that spelled eternity for one of them.

He said, "I always claimed Poco St. Vrain was bogus. I'll prove it."

"Sure," Poco drawled gently. He waited.

Kate watched them both. It was Cardowan who first betrayed a movement by the taut muscles in his throat. They flickered a little, and Kate's eyes switched to Poco.

With that swift, rocking ease that was invisible, his hand, wrist hinged, swung up, gun level, steadied, paused, so that she had time to identify its outline, then exploded.

Cardowan's guns were not clear of leather. They never got clear. He folded both his arms across his chest as Poco shot. Cardowan's back bowed. He screamed, and it bowed some more. The last shot of Poco's drove Cardowan's body finally off balance. His legs left the platform, and, his back a fulcrum against the rail, they lifted and he went over backward, sloping down to the side.

He disappeared. Immediately there was a bump of the wheel on the track, and Kate ran into Poco's outstretched arms.

He held her tight. She was sobbing wildly, terribly, but he was smiling. He held her that way for perhaps half a minute, then she turned her head and kissed him.

"I—" she began.

And he cut in with, "I know. Don't say it."

When she smiled up at him, he took her arms from him gently and said, "We have to get off this, darling. I don't want to die now."

She said, "I don't care."

Poco looked ahead. They were swinging down the long grade into Christian City. Poco turned into the car and yanked open the door of a locker. Lying on a shelf was the brakie's club. He got it, swiveled down the slack in the wheel, inserted the club between the spokes, and again the brakes screamed. But the car, in that long roll, had gained a terrific momentum, one that he knew he could never overcome.

He said to Kate, "Pull those tarps inside in the middle of the car," while he threw his weight against the braking club until his temples seemed ready to split wide open. Kate dragged the gold down the corridor.

Poco saw that they were swinging down onto the short level that took them into the town. The brakes were wailing in a wild scream as the car thundered into the straight stretch headed for the tie bumper at the end of the station platform. It could not be stopped, and Poco knew it.

He said to Kate, "Swing over the rail and wait for me!"

Smiling, Kate did as she was bid.

Just as they were nearing the station, Poco dropped the club, and swung over the rail.

"This will hurt," he said quietly, taking her hand. "The station platform's clear and level with us. Jump when I tell you." He looked at her. "Afraid?"

"Not with you," Kate answered quietly, and then they swung beside the station.

Poco waited a second, then said, "Jump!"

They jumped at the same time, Poco slipping his hand around her waist.

When they landed, Poco hugged her to him, felt himself lose his balance and then the crash, a breath-driving, thudding, skidding, burning, crash, just as the splitting timbers of the bumper boomed in a savage splintering of wood.

Poco, holding her closely, pressing her head into his shoulder, felt the hurt, felt them rolling blindly, and then he was brought up against the wall abruptly, with a force that seemed to crush his bones.

He lay there a minute, fighting for breath, feeling Kate's sucking gasps for air. Then he whispered, "Are you all right?"

She nodded her head and held him close, just as the first man on the scene shouted, "My God, they're dead!"

CHAPTER TWENTY-THREE

Van was in the lead, Cooper behind him, a posseman behind him. They kept to the tracks and rode into the station, and Van pulled up his almost foundered horse.

The runaway car had smashed through the bumper, gouged great twin furrows in the ground for fifty yards, then one furrow disappeared, leaving only the one which was deeper yet. And there, on its side, a great scar torn in the ground, lay the coach in the middle of the main street. Townspeople stood around it.

"Dead," Van said bleakly, and spurred his horse.

The crowd made way for them and Van walked up to the wreck, Cooper by his side. There stood Poco St. Vrain, a girl beside him, a man, Kate's father, beside her. Poco's shirt was ripped almost off and a great bloody weal covered one arm. He grinned at Van, took his gun out and tendered it to him.

"Your gold's inside the car, Lawman. I told you I'd return it. Here are my guns." And with a faint smile he turned to Kate while Van only stared. "Van, this is Mr. Shayne, McCandless's manager." When he had introduced Cooper to Shayne, he took hold of Kate's arm.

"This is my wife," he said quietly, looking soberly at Kate, and added to Van, "That is, she will be if you'll give me time to get married before you jail me."

"I—" Van began, then his voice trailed off. Poco had caught sight of one of the possemen who had caught up with the army, and had ridden all afternoon in chase.

Poco said softly, "Wait a minute." He passed Sam Van and, in passing, flicked up one of Van's guns, and the smack of it was hard in his palm.

He confronted the posseman. "What happened to Steamboat, you?" he asked gently.

The posseman backed up. "She's all right, St. Vrain. She ran out of shells and we rushed the place and found her."

"Is that right?" Poco asked another posseman.

"Sure," the man said quickly.

Poco turned and tossed the gun to Van, and said nothing.

Van said, "Let's go somewhere where we can talk."

Cooper set a guard of soldiers around the gold, and they went into the hotel lobby—Cooper, Shayne, Van, Kate and Poco.

Kate took a deep leather chair and Poco sat on the arm of it. Van drew up a chair, his gentle, thoughtful eyes on Kate. Cooper stood beside Shayne.

"I think I understand now," Van said to Poco, and Poco only smiled.

Van sat down. "Mr. Shayne, you arranged to have this gold shipped, didn't you?"

"Yes. I signed the papers."

Van nodded. "Where are the men the company sent?"

Poco said, "Dead." He explained the killing of Shelton and Finger, one by Cardowan in a stage holdup, the other by a hard-case named Conaghan, at Silver City.

"And where were you?" Van asked.

"I was over at a fiesta in Sacaton county for one week."

"Can you prove that?"

"A hundred people can."

Van said, "Then I don't see that you're responsible for the death of the men."

"Who said I was?"

"But you stole the gold?"

Poco nodded gravely.

"And you got it back, didn't you?"

Again Poco nodded.

Van sighed and said, "It would be a mighty queer outfit that would jail you for that. You killed Cardowan. We saw his—well, we saw him on the tracks. He had stolen the gold and you recovered it."

"Wait a minute," Poco said slowly. "I thought you were naming all the laws I broke."

Van's face did not change. "You rescued Miss Shayne from a kidnap, and will collect considerable bounty for Cardowan's death. You rescued me from a mob, you risked your life a dozen times to get the gold back for the insurance company. What charge have they got against you?"

"Stealing it."

"Was it ever found in your possession except when you turned it over to the authorities after you recovered it?"

Poco looked puzzled. "No."

"Was it ever known to be in your possession?"

Poco looked at Kate. "Kate knew it."

"A woman can't testify against her husband. Anyone else?"

"Shayne gave it to us."

Shayne said, "I'll be in Mexico in a week on a new job. I'll refuse to testify, and I'll fight extradition, in case they try it—which they won't."

"Anyone else?" Van asked.

"The men there at the mine."

"They're scattered all over the country," Shayne put in. "It would cost a fortune to find them again, and if they learned the circumstances, the company would have to spend another fortune getting them together."

"Anyone else?"

Poco, bewildered, shook his head.

Van leaned forward and said, "Then I don't see what case they have against you, St. Vrain. Your wife won't testify that you stole it. Shayne won't, because he won't be here. The men won't, because it would cost too much to get them together. The company has every single ounce of gold. Why would they spend money to prosecute a man who's saved them a nice tidy sum of money? You aren't implicated in either of the killings of their agents. I'll testify you helped me to try and recover the gold after saving my life. You've rid the country of the worst outlaw it has ever seen." He leaned back in his chair. "If there's to be any trial, I think you should bring suit to make the company and the public recognize the favors you've done them," he added dryly.

Poco looked from Van to Kate to Shayne to Van again. "You mean I'm free?"

"Not until you ride with me to interview the company and let me tell the story. At least, that's all I'll hold you for." He looked at Cooper. "What about you, Lieutenant?"

Cooper said gravely, "I'd like nothing better than to lay this before the commandant—but the fact remains, your men attacked a government post and tried to take it by force of arms."

"When?" Poco asked.

Cooper named the night.

"Not that night," Kate cut in. "He was with me, in the San Jons."

"It was Cardowan's and Two-Way's men that they had doublecrossed," Poco cut in. "I guessed that much. I'll even hunt up men that can prove it."

Cooper shrugged. "Then nothing remains—except an apology for uncourteous conduct to the commandant, for"—he smiled in spite of himself—"ramming a bill down his throat."

Kate looked up at Poco. Of all people, an apology for anything seemed the strangest coming from his lips, but he looked down at her and smiled.

"Listen to this," he told her, and said to Cooper, "I apologize. I was a wild, hell-raising nuisance, and I beg the major's pardon."

Cooper nodded, and stood up. "He'll accept. He's a good man, and I think he'd like to hear all this story."

"I'll drop by and see him."

"When you return from your session with the company," Van said. He rose and, along with Cooper and Shayne, went out.

Poco looked down at Kate, his face strangely puzzled. "Funny, isn't it, that I never knew how all right most men are until you give them a chance. Look at Van and Cooper."

"But not at all men," Kate said quietly.

"Cardowan?"

Kate nodded, and held his glance. "Poco, do you know there is three thousand dollars coming to you?"

Poco grimaced with distaste. "Head money," he said, thinking of the reward money from Cardowan's death.

Kate slipped her hand into his. "Yes, head money. Let's build something with it, something that will last and grow, something strong and decent!" She smiled at him. "Maybe it will remind us of the time when you were traveling not so far from head money yourself."

"Ranch?"

"Yes, my husband."

Poco smiled down on her. "That's what I want, too, my wife."

Kate laughed softly. "Did you ever ask me to be your wife? Did I ever say I would?"

Poco said, "No. But you've called me your husband. Did you ever ask me to be your husband?"

"No. Will you?"

"Sure. Will you?"

"Sure."

And for once, Poco saw the future as he had always secretly, quietly, and stubbornly hoped it would be—and he felt humble enough to know he could fight and win with her.